The Half-White Album

Lynn and Lynda Miller Southwest Fiction Series
Lynn C. Miller and Lynda Miller, Series Editors

This series showcases novels, novellas, and story collections that focus on the Southwestern experience. Often underrepresented in American literature, Southwestern voices provide unique and diverse perspectives to readers exploring the region's varied landscapes and communities. Works in the series range from traditional to experimental, with an emphasis on how the landscapes and cultures of this distinct region shape stories and situations and influence the ways in which they are told.

Also available in the Lynn and Lynda Miller Southwest Fiction Series:

Girl Flees Circus: A Novel by C. W. Smith

The Half-White Album

CYNTHIA J. SYLVESTER

Albuquerque
University of New Mexico Press

Library of Congress Cataloging-in-Publication Data
Names: Sylvester, Cynthia J., 1963– author.
Title: The half-white album / Cynthia J. Sylvester.
Other titles: Lynn and Lynda Miller Southwest fiction series.
Description: Albuquerque: University of New Mexico Press, 2023. | Series:
Lynn and Lynda Miller Southwest fiction series
Identifiers: LCCN 2022037781 (print) | LCCN 2022037782 (e-book) |
ISBN 9780826364715 (paperback) | ISBN 9780826364722 (e-pub)
Subjects: LCGFT: Novels.
Classification: LCC PS3619.Y557 H35 2023 (print) |
LCC PS3619.Y557 (e-book) | DDC 813/.6—dc23/eng/20220920
LC record available at https://lccn.loc.gov/2022037781
LC e-book record available at https://lccn.loc.gov/2022037782

Founded in 1889, the University of New Mexico sits on the traditional homelands of the Pueblo of Sandia. The original peoples of New Mexico—Pueblo, Navajo, and Apache—since time immemorial have deep connections to the land and have made significant contributions to the broader community statewide. We honor the land itself and those who remain stewards of this land throughout the generations and also acknowledge our committed relationship to Indigenous peoples. We gratefully recognize our history.

Cover design and Illustration by Felicia Cedillos
Interior text design by Isaac Morris
Composed in Baskerville and Scala Sans

For Mom and Dad

In every conceivable manner, the family is link to our past,
bridge to our future.
—*Alex Haley*

I like beautiful melodies telling me terrible things.
—*Tom Waits*

In beauty my mother for you I return.
—*Jeannie J*

Live at the House of Towers

Live at the House at the Edge of the World

Live at the House of Red Clay

The Covers formed in 1963. The year Patsy Cline and Kennedy died. They like to say they've been on the road so long, they put the "mad" in nomad.

The Covers are:

> Jeannie J: lead vocals, cow bell, and tambourine
> M. R. (Mister): acoustic, electric, and slide guitars
> One Foot: drums and percussion
> Akeedee'naghai'igii: bass guitar
> The New Mexico Women's Correctional Facility Choir: backup vocals on "Brain Damage"

Without music, life would be a blank to me.

—*Jane Austen*

This is what I want in heaven . . . words to become notes
and conversations to be symphonies.

—*Tina Turner*

The House of Towers was downtown. If you didn't know it was there, you'd never find it. That seemed to be the case when we pulled in that night. Even though we were running late, there were only three cars in the parking lot. A storm had followed us since we left Thoreau, and now it sat over our heads as the Econoline shuddered to a stop. Then the sky cracked open, and we saw the back door. It looked like a giant silver tooth in an otherwise empty mouth. Mister had a bad feeling, but we're the Covers. We're like the postman, come rain or shine. So with zigzagged lightning all around us, we grabbed some of our gear and ran toward the door.

—*One Foot*

Live at the House of Towers

COMFORTABLY NUMB

She walked slowly and softly around the sturdy oak table in the formal dining room. The claw-foot pedestal legs seemed particularly vicious this time of the month. A delicate lace tablecloth was barely visible beneath a pile of bills slit open at their sides with the precision of a butcher and situated on the table in a constellation that made sense only to her, as the Pythagorean theorem or the law of relativity does to some, as a recipe for pineapple upside-down cake does to others. Something can be made of it, but only by certain people.

A letter opener her brother-in-law brought back from Korea lay next to the freshest bill. The long red tassel had faded over the past forty years, but not the hand-painted picture of a little man who stood in his boat never losing his balance, still hoping for a lucky fishing day.

She took a deep breath, left the dining room, rummaged through the desk in the kitchen. The lamp above the desk had lost its fluted cover and a single bulb burned brightly, exposing a few cobwebs that hung loosely to and from the phone like a flimsy hammock. She opened the drawer and pulled out a pen she already knew didn't work. The ink had dried up years ago: thirty-nine to be exact, if she counted backward from today, past her divorce, through the years. Back when there was a roast beef cooking in that oven that hadn't worked in five years. When her children were outside running in a sky turning pink. Snotty nosed and red cheeked, they'd burst in with her husband returning from work with a similar charcoal-black pen with "U.S. Government" stamped on the side sticking out of his front shirt pocket. If she closed her eyes, she could still smell the Avon aftershave on it. But she simply turned it over in her hand, the same way she turned over the past, never looking at it directly but out of her peripheral vision. She placed it back in the desk drawer along with nubby crayons, rubber bands, paperclips, a watch that hadn't worked in at least two years, a key chain from the Golden Gate Casino, and a small plastic pink high-heel shoe from her daughter's Barbie doll. She'd sold the doll along with Barbie's brunette cousin, Francie, the red-headed Stacey, and Barbie's beach house for ninety-nine dollars to an obese woman whose number she had found in the *Thrifty Nickel.*

She swiped half-heartedly at the cobwebs that blew in front of her, over the 2007 Elvis calendar. The picture was one of her favorites from the "Aloha from Hawaii via Satellite Concert" he'd recorded before that unfortunate heart attack. It really was a better time to clean than to make out bills. It was getting late, and her eyes burned even during the day over the small numbers.

The ancient furnace in the garage kicked on, blowing its warm, dusty breath through the vents in the kitchen. The rumble of it sounded like her son's two-stroke minibike on its way home. Foolish; her children were grown now.

Her stomach drew inward, as it often did this time of the day, when the light faded and the bills began to disappear, devoured by the benevolent lion of a table in the dimming light.

She clutched her stomach unconsciously. Nobody knew what this was like, the feeling in her stomach, not even the doctors who examined her with scopes and radiographs. Maybe the security guard at the entrance to the casino knew, or the server who brought her coffee at her favorite machine, "The Wheel of Fortune," at two in the morning. Maybe they understood that she could feel the subtle temperature change in the machine that was ready to pay. Maybe they had seen her move along them with the deft fingertips of a blind person or a TV evangelist touching the foreheads of the sick. Maybe they knew that tonight could be her lucky night. She had the faith of the little fisherman on the letter opener. She believed that the night swallowed the day, and then there was no past, just a single moment when all was new.

Her car keys hung on the cork message board that said "Welcome." They winked at her as she reached for them and switched off the light. The constellation of bills shifted in the dark of the dining room as she put on her coat.

Outside the evening star twinkled. The neighbor's dog barked as she walked to the gate. Smiling, she said to the dog, "Oh, Mą'ii, you coyote," even though the dog looked to be half-Chihuahua and half-beagle. "You don't like to stay home either." She opened the gate and pulled her car out. She told her own dogs to stay there and watch the place.

But as she drove away, Mą'ii slipped through an opening in his fence, and her dogs followed. They all chased her down the road, barking.

Across the river, her daughter sat bundled up at her weakening fire. The propane tank that fueled it was nearly empty. She held a beer in her gloved hands, watching the evening star get brighter and brighter. She had stared at that star, which wasn't really a star, her whole life. It, in turn, stared back at her, seeming to know her better than she knew herself. At times she felt tethered to it, tied too tightly perhaps. It tugged at a place deep inside her. She tried to bend her ear toward that place, near her navel where she'd been experiencing discomfort.

If only she had done more yoga, Janu Sirsasana pose, and drank less of these—she looked at the *Tecate* and finished it—she could get to that place more easily. "Try meditation," her therapist had suggested. "Fast," a curandera had advised, after a treatment with a raw egg. The fragrance of roses had wafted through the small apartment as the woman rubbed the egg over her naked body. She had sat wrapped in a towel as the curandera cracked the egg open. Its contents slid into a bowl that could just as easily have held Captain Crunch cereal. They had peered at the egg. The curandera looked up at her warily. "You're holding on too tightly." She peered into the same bowl and only saw the beginnings of an omelet.

She fasted, and still her stomach continued to call to her with sharp pains. Not appendicitis, not gallstones, not a heart attack. "You're fine," her doctor had told her, adding kindly, "maybe lose a little weight, and lay off the beer and spicy food." What else was there, she wanted to ask. The doctor gave her a prescription for Prilosec that she never filled.

Fasting, meditating, more Janu Sirsasana, and no red or green chile, but it didn't help. Tears formed in her eyes as she stared at the star, joined now by its relations. They whispered to one another and sizzled in the night sky. She stayed looking until the fire died and the cold drove her in.

The chimes on the back door, the ones she'd picked up at the Goodwill, a little tinkle of bells, made her pause in the kitchen. The sound continued even though the bells weren't moving. Tinkling, like the bells of the sheep as they were herded over the hills at the base of the red mesas where her mother was born. She thought often of her mother's mother, whom she'd never met. She'd passed away in the Albuquerque Indian Hospital with TB before she was born. Her parents had followed the train that took her back home to the Dinétah.

Home.

To her, home smelled like dust and dogs and sweet bread and Caress soap. Like celery and onions sautéing in butter, like smoke twirling up from ashtrays as cards or stories were laid down, like exhaust from minibikes and lawn mowers pushed through weeds, not grass. It tasted like gas siphoned from that same lawn mower to put in her Ford Pinto because she'd come home on empty, again. She laughed out loud.

She'd call her mom. She wanted to tell her the Lobos were playing BYU tomorrow night. They hadn't been to a game together in a long time, because they were both broke. Maybe they could listen to it on KKOB. Maybe they could play UNO or Rummy even though it wasn't much fun with just two people.

The phone rang and rang in her mom's kitchen, rang until she finally hung up. It was nine o'clock. She hoped her mom just hadn't heard the phone because her hearing aids weren't in. Or didn't answer because she still wasn't talking to her daughter, who had suggested, after shuffling through the bills on her mom's table, maybe she should stop going to the casino. In turn, her mother had looked at her daughter's belly and suggested maybe she should stop drinking so much beer.

She turned on the stereo. On Coyote 102.5 Sammy Hagar was singing about where eagles fly. She clicked on the desk lamp. It glowed yellow, illuminating stacks of books and papers on her desk: typed pages in manilla folders, the same stories written and rewritten, books amassed through years—*The Sacred Hoop, Navajo Made Easier, Bad Indians, Spider Woman's Granddaughters, The Second Long Walk, The Half-Blood, Almanac of the Dead,* academic writings, anthologies, novels, collections of short stories and poems, and historical texts including her mom's yearbooks with aged newspaper clippings folded inside. As a whole they had become a hazy collage of words, photos and facts, whispers and memories and dreams she was trying to piece together.

She picked a book from the top of a stack. It was published in 1902. Printed in eight-point font, she rubbed her eyes. She skipped past the captions—CEREMONY AND RITES, SEASON, EXPENSE, ORIGIN—and like a child with a picture book she looked for that one drawing she loved most. Finely detailed, probably done in pencil, it was of a man in loose-fitting pants and shirt with a blanket draped over his shoulders, standing outside a medicine lodge looking east. She knew it was east because the door to the lodge faced that direction, but also she knew that place and that the mesa was to the west.

She looked at the drawing for some time. She'd given up long ago trying to comprehend the complex ceremony described in great detail in the book. It was comprised of hundreds of songs, sacred arts and tools, and stories that took a medicine man a lifetime to learn. To fully understand the ceremony she'd need to understand the worldview, and to understand the worldview she'd need to know the language, and she only knew enough of the Diné language to say, "Pass the salt," "Come and eat," and to introduce herself—to say, "I was born for my mother's, mother's, mother's clan, and we're from this place." If she had colored pencils or crayons, she could fill in the sun descending behind the red sandstone mesa, the coral- and ecru-hued hills speckled with sage and greasewood that rolled into the dunes then spilled into the flat of the wash where corn used to grow. She'd add an elm tree her grandfather planted to shade the little sandstone house. Then it would be the place her mother was born.

She put the book down and typed, "Home."

She wrote that home smelled like dust and dogs and sweet bread and Caress soap. She wrote that it was a place that knew her better than she knew it. She wrote about the fragrance of Russian Olive trees in the spring and alfalfa in the summer, of wood smoke and coffee at dawn, about the sound of sheep bells and the barking of old dogs, about black crows and arrows and shadows, about being dead and not knowing it. Her fingers tapped on the keys like ancient dancers of an even older ceremony performed only in the winter. Moccasined feet lightly touched the ground as her fingers tapped out stories, her songs, her prayers, her offering.

For how many nights, how many years, had she sat and tapped on that keyboard? Her fingers walking a zigzagged path toward a medicine lodge at the base of the red mesas where a supine patient lay on a dry painting made from multicolored sand. The patient could be her. It could be her mom, or her grandmother, or her cousin.

She walked ahead of the medicine women and men who were arriving to administer to seen and unseen wounds, ahead of the day keepers in nurse's scrubs, stethoscopes around their necks with which to monitor the strength of the patient's heart during those winter nights.

She walked to the doors of their many houses with her offering. She walked with the acknowledgement that parts of her were not nizhonidi, not walking in beauty, and with the parts of her that felt chindi or taboo. Tears plopped onto her desk, an offering for the parts of her that felt like they had been struck by lightning.

"This is my sand painting, this paper, black on white. These pieces, poems and stories, are my songs that I offer to the night sky with the hope that at dawn the ancient deities will see me—see us—and remember our names.

"I am Kiyaa'aanii nishłį, Bilagáana bá shíshchíín." Maybe she could walk between worlds, maybe she could walk where lightning had struck and find that the path between black and white and this and that was just the zigzagged path of lightning. Find that they weren't cast out, but lead. Lead to this side of the river and born into this place called Bee'eldíildahsinil—'where the bell sits up high.'"

It is on this zigzagged path she wanders now and looks up into the black sky of her heart, into the hole, and wonders: Will their losses ever be recovered, or is this hole an opening from where the journey begins?

What is the world coming to?

—*Ozzy Osbourne*

I MIGHT HAVE BEEN QUEEN

There are no words in this language to translate her name. A name that stretches back to the time with no time, then flashes forward ten thousand years. But you should know that her name is like the warm touch of fingers on your forearm when you're afraid or lost, that it smells like a late spring morning in the valley when the Russian Olives are in bloom, the coffee done perking; it tastes like the fatty edge of meat—butchered with the knife of a warrior—salty and crisp, flecked with bits of sand that stick between our big white front teeth, sand that blows across the dunes over by the old house, uncovering pottery shards that refuse to remain buried.

BOULEVARD OF BROKEN DREAMS

With a blanket across her broad shoulders and a shawl covering her head. With ants dreaming, still furled on cool sand, sprinkling corn pollen on the path ahead of her,
                          she walked.
Past the well, where the old buzzard still slept, his head tucked under a molted wing, across the dunes, toward the hills emerging from shadow,
                          she walked.
Focusing her mind on moist yellow corn tassels from the abundance of rain in a summer that was almost past, now,
                          she walked.
Shawl tight around her ears, not against the chill of dawn but from the thoughts that crept in like the day was creeping over the hills
                          she walked.
And despite the beauty above her, below her, the beauty all around her, her thoughts turned to the smoke
                that walked   beside her.

Smoke she tried to push away, to think away,
                          as she walked,
across the dunes   to her field of plenty,
                          she walked.

THE LAST ONE

Shimá had started at dawn harvesting, cutting, then grinding kernels of corn into a sweet paste. Now she patted the last of the gooey substance into husks, folding and tying the loaves of bread with tired fingers. She stood slowly, hips and knees sore from kneeling for so long. She looked to the east, hoping to see her husband on his way home. It was work that was supposed to be done with other women, with her daughters, with laughter and song. But her relatives weren't able to come and help, and all her daughters were away. She hadn't complained that her husband was leaving too, making the overnight trip to the trading post. He had taken some of their goods—sheepskins, wool, and two blankets she'd woven—to trade for winter stock. She wasn't upset that he'd left at this time, when the corn was still young and juicy enough to make bread, because he promised that on his way home he'd stop at the mission boarding school and check on their daughters. She was anxious to hear how they were, especially her youngest.

Nothing moved on the horizon. The sparrows held still in the sagebrush, the lizards lazed on hot rocks—even her sheep dogs, a crew of three mutts, were too hot to chase rabbits into their holes. They dozed under greasewoods that provided growing shade as the sun laid down its head on the red mesa. As if on cue, the breeze that always came up with the sunset rustled her long skirt, reminding her in its tickle of cloth on leg to stop worrying and finish the bread before it got dark. To emphasize that point, the old buzzard that hung around at the well began his slow descent. His hollow bones, hopefully, warmed enough to make it through the cool August night.

Shimá picked up the shovel and stirred the coals in the pit fire she'd built at noon. The embers were hot. She removed the larger chunks of wood and placed them on a flat piece of metal she'd found several years ago half buried in the sand dunes. It was the hood of an old car. She and the mule her youngest had named Hell pulled it out and drug it home. As she looked at her earth oven, Shimá thought about what her daughter had told her. That the kitchen at the boarding school was the only thing she liked, that, and the radio in the basement where she worked doing laundry. She said the radio crackled like a fire and hummed with songs that came from far away. And the ovens, the ovens lit with a snap of fingers. She said they made bread with sugar and yeast. Bread that rose up like a big moon over the side of the bowl.

Shimá kneeled at her earth oven, looked at her bread made from ground corn. It had been all-day work, and she had six dozen loaves that looked like faceless dolls, maidens in stiff dresses. She picked up a loaf, looked at it, and said, "Are you little ladies going to rise like the moon under this old hood." Her face burned, and she squinted her eyes against the heat that immediately curled the bottoms of the maiden's dresses as she laid them side by side.

Shimá hummed a song, adding it to the bread. As the sun descended slowly, her song was a sort of lullaby to the little corn-husk ladies, as if they were her children. One by one she put them in the oven, just as her own children had been taken to the mission school, one by one.

Shimá had six daughters, and she had named the last one, The Last One. She did this because she swore that that child would be the last one she'd push out into the world just to be swallowed up by the missionaries or the government. It's not as if she didn't understand that they had to go to school. It's that they took them with the purpose of changing them. Yes, we all change, she agreed with her husband when they argued about the boarding school, but it was how they changed. Each time she took a child there to live she studied them, tried to remember what they had been like, because the next time she saw them their long hair would be cut short, their long skirts and blouses with silver buttons would be replaced with short light-blue dresses, their faces no longer full, their eyes distant.

The Last One was born ornery and independent, so much so that she was more often than not in trouble at home, too. She'd get on a horse that wasn't yet broken, or take the sheep farther than told, so that she and the sheep didn't get home until well after dark. Shimá thought that The Last One would face her new future with that same bravery. But instead, when Shimá took her to the school, she'd clutched Shimá's leg and buried her face in Shimá's skirt to hide her tears. Shimá had knelt in front of her and whispered into the top of her sweet, sweaty head, "Shhh." She had pointed to the mesa that was behind her now. "If you stand right here and look that way. See? Right there, that's where you're from. You'll see the smoke from my fire, and I can see you, so be good. Be strong," she'd told her, and herself. Little did she know that her daughter would stand at that spot every day looking for smoke.

Smoke rose up from the coals now, as Shimá pulled the hood over the pit, over the little ladies. "I'll see you soon." She stood and dusted dirt from her skirt. The dogs had snuck off while she loaded the oven, and now they barked from the other side of the hill. It was the bark usually reserved for her daughter. The Last One.

She called for them. They ran toward her as a mule with a rider plodded over the hill. The dogs circled Shimá then took off once again. In the saddle was a small man, and behind him rode a child. A girl. Shimá dropped her shovel.

Even though they were still a distance away, she knew it was her, and her heart dropped into her stomach. She was supposed to be at school. They—Shimá, The Last One, and Claude, Shimá's husband—had all been warned less than a month ago that if she ran away again, they, the government, would send her farther away. Shimá looked around to see if anyone else was coming, thankful that as far as the eye could see there was nothing and that the long shadow of the mesa was beginning to cover them. She walked to the trough and began to pump the well until she could hear Slim singing and could see The Last One's blue school dress bunched up past her knees. Her brown legs dangled, socks loose at her ankles, school boots untied. The mule upped his gait to a trot, which roused her daughter. She lifted her head, saw Shimá at the well, and slid off the mule, dropped to the ground, and ran to her mother. She hugged her. Shimá placed her hand on the top of her head, rubbed her cheek, and turned down the white collar of her dress, still as stiff as a corn husk.

"What are you doing here?" Shimá asked. The Last One dug her strong hands into Shimá's waist.

Shimá and Slim nodded in greeting.

He removed his sweat-stained hat. "I found your daughter walking alone in the wash like a stray dog." The mule stuck his nose into the water, and The Last One rubbed his sweaty neck. Shimá pumped a ladle of water for Slim. He took it, his brown hands weathered and arthritic. His chest and hips were a little bonier then the last time Shimá had seen him.

After a long drink, Slim said, "Claude's on his way back."

Shimá didn't ask where he'd seen him. Slim was known for wandering around looking for card games.

As if he could read her mind, he laughed. "At the trading

post—working." He took on a stern face, unnatural for him, and pointed the empty ladle at The Last One. "I told her, she's going to get lost out there." He directed the ladle to the hills that rolled one after the other toward the Chuska Mountains. "Or the coyotes will track her down like a sheep and get her. She said she wasn't scared." He shook his head.

"I'm not," The Last One said.

He pointed the ladle at her again. "I told her then they'll send her away. Far away, where she won't find her way back so easy. Like my grandson. You know what she said to that?" He handed the ladle back to Shimá. The mule picked his wet nose up out of the trough, as if he were listening too. "She said that the smoke from her mother's fire would always find her." The mule snorted, shooting water and mucus onto The Last One's blue dress.

Shimá looked at her daughter, who was looking at the mule, who was looking at Shimá. "That's what they told her. We told her too. And now he's telling, you, Daughter. Tsk." She didn't want to think about how she had made it as far as the wash. The school was over thirty miles away. She had run away three times now. The first time, she'd hidden in the back of one of the school's trucks headed to the trading post at Kayenta and walked the last ten miles home. The last time, Shimá was informed by her in-laws that The Last One had been helped by an old woman on an even older horse. That time it took them nine days to get her back to the school. She had been gone so long that the officials were glad to see she hadn't been killed or eaten or . . .

"Kidnapped!" Slim said. "Back in my day, the Mexicans might kidnap you, or the Apaches might take off with you, or leave you and take your horse, or worse yet, you might get found by the soldiers and taken to the Place of Sorrow."

A small vein was beginning to stick up on Slim's forehead, raising up despite the indentation from his hat band. Shimá rubbed the mule's neck. "We've told her and told her."

"She thinks she knows. She's stubborn like Claude."

"Father said it was Mother that was stubborn."

"Shhh," Shimá said. "Go get Slim some corn. Go!" She watched her run, waiting for her to trip over her untied shoelaces. She turned to Slim, "I don't know what to do." She felt like burying her face in the long neck of the stinking mule and crying. But she didn't. Instead she asked Slim to stay for dinner. "It's too late to be out wondering around. Your wife would be angry with you." His wife had passed ten years earlier from tuberculosis.

"There's a dance not too far from here."

The Last One ran back with the corn in a burlap sack. She handed it to her mother, who put it in the saddlebag on the mule.

"They sent my grandson to Carlisle," he told her. "He liked to run around with me, so I guess it's for the best." He tried to laugh.

Shimá didn't think that at all. "Thank you, Slim. Thank you for bringing my daughter home." She knew there wasn't anyone around for miles. No dances, no poker games.

"Tell Claude to come see me this winter." He smiled, only a few teeth left. He was one of the few men who still knew how to play the Moccasin Game. "Tell him to bring one of your blankets and some sheepskins." He laughed, then began to cough. He rubbed the mule behind one long ear and nudged his belly with his short legs. The mule didn't budge. "Nobody listens to me anymore," he said. He pulled the reins to one side, and the mule knew it was no use and turned his head toward the road. Slim clicked his tongue, then looked at Shimá, "They'll come for her."

Shimá placed her hand on top of The Last One's head, and they watched him and the mule head back onto the road and away from her home. She tried to smooth The Last One's hair down, but her rebellion was in her hair. It stuck up like a puppy's. Shimá took water and smoothed it, the bangs sticking to her damp forehead. "I should have named you Fuzzy Head." Then she knelt and hugged her. She wiped the dust from her face with the hem of her skirt. It was just her and her daughter, and the old buzzard. The dogs would follow Slim for a while, hoping he'd drop some food.

"You heard him. Didn't you? You can't keep doing this." She should tell her now. You know you have to go back. You know that you can't stay. She should scold her, dole out punishment. But those words were too hard right now. And how would she punish her further? The worst punishment for her was already what she would get whether she behaved or not. She watched her daughter pick up a stink bug. She was ten now, but she still liked bugs and dogs and mules. The bug crawled up her arm. Shimá looked closely. It left little yellow marks on her daughter's brown arm. Corn pollen. It must have traveled along the pollen trail Shimá had made that morning when she went to her field to harvest, sprinkling pollen in front of her. Maybe it was a good sign. Maybe . . . she thought . . .

She took her daughter's hand and they walked to the house. "You're lucky your father isn't here."

"I'd be sleeping with the sheep tonight."

Thankfully it was getting dark so The Last One couldn't see Shimá smile. "With the goats."

They walked past the oven.

"When will your bread be ready?"

"Soon."

Shimá hoped that baking under an August twilight wouldn't make the little maidens taste like longing.

Shimá made The Last One fetch water for a bath, and she heated it on the woodstove. Juniper popped and cracked. She made her daughter sit still in the tub long enough to wash her feet and scrub under her nails. Shimá scrubbed her head for her while she squirmed. The light from the oil lamp flickered, casting dancing shadows on the walls in the sandstone cabin. Shimá watched her daughter dress. Her skinny ankles stuck out from the bottom of the long skirt as she pulled the blouse over her head, smoothed it against her flat chest, and smiled. "This is my favorite."

The dogs barked, and The Last One went to the door. She stopped abruptly.

They looked at each other.

"Your father."

Claude entered in his usual way, pushing open the door while carrying an armful of wood, a shoulder bag full of dried meat, and a canteen. He placed everything in its proper place—by the stove, on the table, and he hung the canteen on a peg, followed by his hat and coat. Shimá watched him act as if there were nothing wrong, nothing out of place, or more like there was something there that shouldn't be. He blew out his breath and said, "Hello, hello, it was a long ride." He smelled of horse and dust. "I got a whole bag of beans and a sack of flour, and bright-red yarn." He pulled this out of the saddlebag. "For your weavings, and you have orders for more." He spoke of the two blankets Shimá had woven this past spring. She was working on another now. It hung on the loom, nearly complete. "It took me two days to get here because everywhere I stopped there was a relative. 'Claude, I haven't seen you, come in.' 'Claude, why haven't you been by? How's your wife?' 'She's at home angry with me I'm sure, because I'm here, and she's working hard as usual.'" He stopped and looked at her, but he had yet to even look at or directly speak to The Last One, who sat at the table with her hands folded.

He poured water in the enamel basin that sat atop a crude wooden stand, took up a bar of soap, and lathered his hands. "She's harvesting, I told my relatives. 'I take it, since you all are still here, and she's not, that none of you went to help her, and she's going to be even angrier with me because now she'll know, because one of you will tell her, that I'm out here wandering around eating mutton stew and sitting at your warm fire.'" He only stopped talking long enough to wash his face, making bubbling noises that made The Last One look less tense. By the time he finished, the front of his shirt was damp and his broad face was clean, smelling of soap. His back was to the table and their daughter. He glanced at Shimá, who handed him a towel.

"Are you angry with me?" he asked her. He turned and looked at his daughter and spoke to her for the first time. "Should she be angry with me?"

The Last One shook her head.

"Well," he pulled a wrapped object out of his pocket and held it out to Shimá. He was shorter than her. He liked to tell the girls that it was a hot day when he'd met their mother. He liked to say he'd fallen in love with her shadow. She took the gift from his damp hand, hands too large for his body, square, and, despite all his hard work, soft. "Nobody came to help you. Nobody but our daughter."

The wood in the stove popped and the water boiled. Shimá took the gift and placed it on the washstand, picked up a fork, and turned her back to both of them. She flipped the meat, and it sizzled. Shimá turned to look at him. He gave her a sad smile, and she nodded her head toward the table. "I'm sure you're hungry from all your galivanting."

He took a deep breath. "I am. I am. And it smells wonderful." Claude placed his hands on his flat belly. He looked like he'd lost five pounds since he'd left only a few days earlier. He told her that he'd been able to pick up some work at the trading post unloading shipments. That's what had kept him. She knew he wasn't galivanting. He was a hard worker. He'd worked to make a home for them that they could stay in summer and winter. No more moving from higher to lower ground to feed the sheep or get out of hot weather or move to warmer weather. He'd built them this house of stone. The same stone that the mission school was made from. Chiseled block by block from the mesa and hauled here by their two mules, the ones The Last One renamed Heaven and Hell. The door unlatched and creaked open. Shimá went to shut it. She saw the hills, dark silhouettes against the sky, soon to disappear. With no moon tonight, she'd need to take a lamp to retrieve her bread later.

Claude sat across the small table from The Last One. It rocked slightly as he rested his arms on it. The room was filled with the yellow glow of the oil lamp, and it seemed like a warm scene that any mother would hope for.

"Hello, Father."

Shimá placed a cup of coffee in front of him, put her hand on his shoulder, and squeezed it before returning to the stove.

"Thank you." He added two scoops of sugar and stirred. He blew on it. Set it down in front of him, rubbed his broad face. He had no whiskers, and Shimá noticed creases were beginning to form at the corners of his dark, nearly black eyes. He was becoming chiseled like the stone of their house, by his own hand, his hard work, and the sun and the wind.

He picked up his cup again and took a sip, put it back down, and kept his hands curled gently around the mug. "Guess who I saw on the way home?" The Last One said nothing. "Slim. You know he's always talking about selling me that mule of his. I made him an offer, and he says he'll think about it." He took a sip, added more sugar. "Then he tells me, only after haggling more about that mule, that my youngest daughter was home from school. Impossible, I just took her back three weeks ago."

A big tear rolled down The Last One's cheek. She took a note out of the waistband of her skirt. Shimá looked over her shoulder at it. It was a note written in English with a pencil. She recognized one of the few English words she knew: "Ruth," the name the missionaries had given The Last One.

"It says I do not have to go back to school anymore. They said I could stay here and help my mother." She placed it on the table, smoothed it with her small brown hand. She pushed the note toward her father, who didn't read or speak English either, but both he and Shimá had seen enough of the bilagánna's official letters to know this had been written by a child, their child. "They said I could stay."

Shimá saw her husband's face drop. He didn't know what to do either. But still he began the same talk he'd given her the last time. The same talk that Slim had given her, that she had given her. That there was no choice and they were lucky that the school took her back the last time, and lucky that the school was as close as it was . . .

Shimá slammed the door to the stove shut. "Lucky," she said out loud. Both The Last One and her husband looked at her.

"Get the plates," she directed her daughter, "I've got to get my bread."

"I'll help you," The Last One said.

"Fix your father's plate." Shimá lit another lamp, then took a blanket and draped it over her shoulders.

Outside the stars were cold and distant. The chill in the air despite it being late August always surprised her, usually delighted her after a hot day. She set the lamp at the edge of the pit and retrieved the pans to put the bread in. She took the shovel and pushed the metal aside. The heat rose from the earth. She considered her daughter's "note from the school." Under different circumstance they would have thought it was funny, laughed privately, that their daughter had made up one of the stories she was always telling them. Stories like the one about the billy goat who only had one horn because he was so gluttonous and ornery that instead of eating grass, he ate a prairie dog. The only way for the prairie dog to get out of the ornery goat was to chew off one of his horns from the inside and crawl out the hole. "Just like we had to climb out the hole from the third world into this one." Just like they seemed to be crawling into a new one now.

Shimá knelt above her little ladies in their brown corn-husk dresses and wept.

The dress, the color of blue-jay eggs, dried stiffly above the woodstove. By the door was The Last One's polished school boots and a pair of mended socks. Hanging on a peg by the door was a saddlebag stuffed with loaves of bread and a single piece of hard candy, white and red waves of sugar almost too pretty to eat. Shimá had been saving it to give to her daughter for Christmas.

Claude quietly came back inside. He'd fed, then hitched the mules to the wagon. It was still dark out, and as Shimá turned to look at him, she saw the morning star dangling. The chill air that followed Claude in the cabin was driven back by the heat from the stove that Shimá had kept going all night. Coffee boiled. Corn mush gurgled and was ready to serve.

Claude stood beside her. "I don't want her to go either."

Shimá put mugs on the table. Placed a bowl next them and glopped mush into it.

"They have to learn their language. Take me for example. I can only go so far because I don't know their language."

"How far do you want to go?" Shimá said as she globbed another spoonful into his bowl. She'd overcooked it, and it stuck to the spoon. "And do not lecture me one more time on things that you don't have or don't understand. You, and them," she pointed the spoon to someplace outside of the walls of their home, "are cut from similar cloth. Always thinking about what is beyond this. Don't lie to yourself, Claude. They take our children because they think we, I, am too backward to care for them properly. Yes, they teach them English. They also teach them to forget their language, their home." She turned away from him. "To forget me. Will my grandchildren even know my name?"

"Here, let me have that." He reached to take the spoon and the pan of mush from her, but she pulled away and set it on the stove. "Sit down. Let's talk before I go."

Shimá sat. "The last time I saw our oldest daughter at the school, I called her by the name *we* gave her, and she said to only call her Rachel now." She tapped her finger on the table. "I know your arguments about living in the past, but I am not the past. I am their mother. I know there is much in this world I don't understand. I accept that. I accept that I don't have an oven that lights like that." She snapped her fingers. "I don't know how to make Moon Bread or play the organ so that my songs travel beyond these hills. But someday, someday, my daughters will need my songs, my stories, and they will have been forgotten. And then what will they do?" She looked at The Last One, who still slept soundly on the cot.

Claude stirred his coffee, sprinkled sugar over his corn mush. "What do you want to do? Should we sell the herd. Board up this house and move to live near the school? I can work at the trading post and you can too. You can weave rugs in the storefront while the tourists watch."

"Have you ever heard the stories told in this book?" She pointed to the Black Book. She'd gotten it out last night and looked at the picture of a woman kneeling by a great river, placing a bundled child in a basket. "She doesn't know where her child is going. I do know how far my child is away from me. Only the length of my thumb on that map you showed me. But when they come back, I can tell by their eyes, they've been much farther away than that." Shimá pointed to the engraving again. "She's saving her child by letting it go. I hope that's what we are doing, too."

She got up from the table.

"My fear is that if she keeps this up, they won't take her back. Then what will we do?"

Shimá turned around. "You give them more. More money. More sheep. More of my blankets. You give them our apologies. We'll get down on our knees like the woman at the banks of the river."

Shimá walked to the stove and got The Last One's dress. It was warm. She went to the bed and gently woke her daughter. She wiped her hair from her eyes and placed the dress on the bed. "You need to get up."

The Last One sat and looked around. She blinked the sleep from her eyes. She saw the dress. Saw her father eating his breakfast. "You're taking me back."

Shimá nodded.

"Let them just forget about me. They'll just forget."

"No, they won't. The more you run, the more they look." She took her hand. "Get dressed and come and eat."

"No."

Shimá took a deep breath. She folded the dress neatly and put it in the saddlebag. "You can change before you get to the school."

"No."

"Do as we say," Claude stood.

"No."

"I'm done explaining things to you," Claude said. "Now let's go."

The Last One ran to her mother. "Please don't make me."

Shimá got her heavy blanket. She walked to her daughter and wrapped it around her shoulders. She knelt in front of her, she kissed her, then she picked her up and carried her to the wagon. The Last One kicked and screamed and begged. Claude got on the buckboard, and Shimá handed her to him. The Last One sat with the blanket caught under her, cocooned inside of it. The world seemed at this moment a giant bird with black wings watching them.

"Shhh," Shimá said. "Listen. Listen to me, little caterpillar. I have a job for you." Shimá knew how much her daughter loved to work with her. Loved to be by her side. She had to swallow her tears as she looked at her. "I need for you to tell your sisters to come home for harvest." Often times children that were not delinquents and who had parents that could go to the school and get them were allowed to go home for a few days in the fall to help with moving the sheep or to finish the work that needed to be done before winter. "We'll come for all of you."

"When?" The Last One asked.

"Near the Harvest Moon. That's not too long."

The Last One cast her eyes down. "You're just saying that to get rid of me."

"I would love nothing more than for you to stay right here with me. But you can't, and you have to promise me to be good. You have to promise me that you won't run away again. If you do, you won't be able to help me. Do you understand? I can't do all this by myself." She swept her arm around. "Besides, your father and I need for you to teach us English, so we can get the best deals for our wool and my blankets. Okay." She rubbed her daughter's forehead. It was so soft. "One day I'll teach you how to weave, and you'll teach me how to make Moon Bread. Okay."

Tears streamed down The Last One's face.

"Now, let me go and get you some bread, and there is a surprise in the bag."

"What surprise?"

Claude put his arm around The Last One and pulled her to him. The air was so cold, so sharp. She tried to catch her breath as she walked back into the house. She put bread in the bag, stuffed it as full as she could. Then carefully, in a little brown sack, she put more ribbon candy and a big fat juicy orange. She doubled over with a stabbing pain in her stomach. She held to the back of the chair until it subsided. Straightening herself, she returned to the wagon.

Claude held out his hand for the bag as mother and daughter looked at one another. Shimá wondered if that little baby the other woman had put in the river ever forgave his mother for letting him go.

She let go of the bag, and her baby was again afloat in a great river. She stood and watched the wagon as it made its way to the rutted road. Toward the rising sun. She thought she heard her daughter screaming for her, but it was just the crows cawing, moving south for the start of their day. Shimá went back in the house. Her coffee was cold. She opened the Black Book that she'd set on the table, the book that Beatrice the missionary had given her in exchange for her daughters.

It was embossed with gold letters. HOLY BIBLE.

Shimá opened it to the back. She rubbed a finger over the words written there under "Baptisms." She worked to pronounce the strange names. Her daughter's new names. Rachel. Sarah. Mary. Leah. Eve. Ruth.

Shimá stood back and looked at the rug on the loom. She ran her hand over the weaving. She'd put all her energy into this one, weaving late into the night. It was fall now, and this was her third rug this year. Her husband told her that her work was sought after. She was meticulous, refusing to have lumpy blankets or rugs. She often combined her best yarn with the Germantown yarn shipped to the trading post from Pennsylvania. Her husband showed her patterns popular with the tourists who had made their way by train or car to the outskirts of Dinétah. They called it Indian Country. That was fine. They paid more.

She opened the cabin door to let more light in and saw their wagon approaching. Just as she had promised, Claude had gone to get her three daughters that were still at the school. The oldest three had already graduated and decided they wanted to see the world. One was in California, one in New Mexico, and the other, she wasn't sure. She hadn't heard from her in nearly a year.

But these three were home to help with the harvest and to visit their mother. She saw two thin figures beside her husband. The Last One must be in the back. Hiding. She loved to play tricks. Shimá smiled, wrapped her blanket around her shoulders, and went to meet them at the well.

The two older girls jumped off the buckboard, the smaller of the two falling to her knees in the sand. They ran to the well. The old buzzard was perched on the long pipe running to the trough. He lifted his carrion head from between his shoulders and stared at them with red-rimmed eyes. The older daughter, Sarah, tried to scare the large bird away by waving her arms and throwing a rock. The bird dipped his bald head toward them and opened his wings, nearly as wide as Rachel was tall. They screamed, dropped the ladle they were drinking from, and ran hand-in-hand toward the corral to check on their lambs that weren't lambs anymore. Shimá yelled at them to wait. They called, "We'll be back."

Claude let the mules water, pumping water in the trough. He didn't look up, and The Last One didn't jump off the back of the wagon to surprise her. Claude looked at her and shook his head. Her knees nearly gave way. She looked in the back of the wagon. Potatoes, beans, flour. No daughter.

"Where is she?"

He didn't answer her.

"Where is my daughter?"

He took his hat off and held it in his hands. "She wasn't there. She ran away two days ago."

Shimá held to the side of the wagon, her chest tight, that pain in her stomach, stabbing. "Sarah and Rachel? They don't know anything about it?" She had told them to take care of their sister.

"If they do, they're not saying. Don't be angry with them. It's not their fault. They can't keep track of her night and day. Nobody can."

She looked toward the hills where she'd seen her last, riding away in the wagon, looking back at her.

Shimá turned and walked back to the house.

She prepared lamb and fry bread. She stirred the pumpkin soup to keep it from burning. *She'll be home.*

She didn't hear Claude walk in. When she turned, he was standing at her loom, back toward her. In the dim light of the cabin, the rug seemed to hang of its own volition.

He murmured, "It's beautiful."

The background was light gray, the color of the sky before it snows, while the two central designs in the foreground moved from brightest white, lighter, then abruptly changed to red and then to black. The designs were not exactly diamond shaped or the sun symbol that would later be called a swastika, but rather Shimá's artistic hybrid of the two, made in such a way that they looked like whirlwinds spinning, one clockwise and the other counterclockwise. The border was a combination of black and gray zigzags of lightning. Her husband rubbed his dusty hands on his pant leg and stepped nearer to the rug, looking closely at the details. He gently felt its smooth fabric, searching for the imperfection he knew she had woven into it. Only on close observation could it be found in the very eye of the storm, a nearly imperceptible change in the color of the yarn, and slightly raised, creating the effect in sight and touch that there was something holding still in the center of the whirlwind.

"Even your imperfections are perfect," he told Shimá. He took a long drink of water she offered him. "Rachel and Sarah will be here the rest of the week. I'll eat and then go look for her."

A silence that had grown inside Shimá and spread out between her and her husband since The Last One was sent back to school seemed to crackle now like the slabs of meat in the frypan that were burning. She left them to burn. She didn't care. Her insides felt like the design in the rug, spinning this way and that.

"She'll make it home," Claude told her, tried to take hold of her arm.

She walked out to the wagon and said, not to her husband but to the magenta sky, "And then what?"

The Last One did make it home. She showed up near evening the next day. Claude and Slim had gone to look for her. Rachel and Sarah were bringing the sheep and goats in from grazing. The barking of the dogs and the jingle of the bell on her oldest sheep carried easily through the cold, thin air. There would be a heavy frost tonight, and she'd already told the girls that they would need to get the rest of the pumpkins in or they'd ruin. She had just finished hitching the mules when she saw her, a blue dot moving across the hills of greasewood and sagebrush. Rachel and Sarah saw her, too. They ran toward their sister, the dogs following them. The sheep walked lazily toward what was left of Shimá's cornfield.

Sarah took off her jacket and wrapped it around her youngest sister. Rachel pulled her toward the well and got her some water. They were too far away for Shimá to hear what they were saying, but she hoped Sarah was telling her how angry their father had been. And that Rachel was telling her, as she wiped her face, that he and Shimá had fought about what to do with her. Shimá had had time to think about what she'd say when she saw her. She'd rehearsed her anger, but as each hour passed and The Last One wasn't home yet, she said when she did see her, she'd hug her and feed her and then—who knew? She didn't have time to get that far.

As Rachel and Sarah put their arms around The Last One's shoulders and led her to the house, Shimá saw dust rising from the other side of the dunes. It was either several riders on horseback coming fast, or a car driving slowly. No matter which, something was headed their way. The dogs saw it too and ran ahead to find out.

The Last One ran to meet her mom. Her lips were cracked and eyes rimmed red like the old buzzard. She was skinnier than that last time she'd seen her. Her hair stuck up like she'd been struck by lightning. Shimá looked toward the dust cloud. "Get the sheep in." The Last One went to help her sisters, but Shimá caught her arm and pulled her toward the house.

"Mother, you're not going to believe this, but I was in the basement when Father came. Working my fingers to the bone. Laundry for the pastor. The teachers were so upset I missed him, because I have been so good. So they said for me to go after him. 'He's just over at the trading post,' but I—"

Shimá closed the cabin door, turned and looked at her. "Stop it! All you've learned how to do in that school is to listen to the radio and to lie." She closed the damper of the stove. "Do you understand how much your father and I worry?" She looked around the room, retrieved the rug she had taken off the loom. "You're not thinking of anyone but yourself."

"What are you doing?" The Last One asked. She started backing up toward the door. "Mother, please."

Sarah rushed in the door. "They're coming."

Shimá went to the door and saw for herself the swirl of dust, tinged with smoky-blue exhaust.

Shimá took a deep breath. "Finish helping Rachel with the herd."

"What are you going to do?" Sarah asked, holding to The Last One's arm, afraid she was going to run outside.

She held her face still. "We're going to get the pumpkins up. So, hurry."

Sarah ran out the door and toward the corral. Shimá handed The Last One a piece of bread. "Stay in here. I mean it."

The Last One nodded.

Shimá took several blankets out to the wagon, pulled the reins of the mules hard enough that neither Heaven nor Hell thought to try and disobey her. She brought the wagon around to the front of the cabin. With long strides she went back in, put bread and dried beef in one saddlebag, filled a canteen with water. She handed these to The Last One. Shimá looked at her. Smoothed her puppy-dog hair, then picked up the rug and draped it over her long arm. She pulled The Last One in close beside her, and they walked out the door. The car wasn't to the well yet. She held the rug up and told The Last One to lay down in the back. "Stay still."

The Last One did as she was told, and Shimá placed the heavy rug on top of her. Her daughter disappeared under the swirling pattern.

Shimá climbed onto the seat of the buckboard. From that height she could see clearly the car bumping along. Inside the car two heads lolled side to side like rag dolls. She slapped the reins on the rumps of the mules. Again they did what was asked of them without hesitation. The wagon rocked forward. Rachel and Sarah ran toward her from the corral. She stopped for them, then proceeded toward the road and the oncoming car. The hills glinted with mica as the sun began to set behind the mesa.

Rachel and Sarah looked back at the house. "Where is she?"

"Shhh," Shimá said. "Turn around. Don't look back."

Shimá could hear the car now, clacking and squeaking like it might fall apart. Shimá could see the driver turning the wheel side to side, trying to stay out of the ruts. The mules paid it no attention and headed straight toward it.

Rachel whispered, "It's the administrator. What are you going to do, Mother? You can't keep her."

Sarah hissed at her sister, "Don't be a snitch."

"I'm not."

"You are. Always trying to get on their good side."

The car and the wagon met, the car sputtering to a stop. The mules stood high above the hood. The driver got out. The passenger, a woman, got out too. It was Beatrice the Missionary, Maker of Moon Bread in the Magic Kitchen with the Black Book on her table.

Shimá sat tall. They greeted one another. "Ya-at-ehs" and "Hellos" exchanged.

"That road isn't meant for man or beast," the administrator said, looking back at it. He took off his hat and dusted his pants and jacket with it. In response Hell sneezed. Beatrice took off her scarf despite the chill in the air. Her hair was short like her daughter's hair was now.

"It's good to see you," Beatrice said, looking at Rachel to translate for Shimá.

Shimá smiled.

The administrator looked at Rachel, and they discussed something. Shimá heard The Last One's missionary name, Ruth. Rachel nodded, then she said to Shimá, "I told them that you knew The Last One had run away again."

Shimá nodded.

He talked more. Looking at Shimá. A long discussion ensued between Rachel and the administrator. Finally, Rachel said, "He wants to know if you know where she is."

She looked at him, then at Beatrice, and got down and went to the back of the wagon. She thought about her husband and his ability to change with the times. She thought about Old Man Slim's grandson. She wondered if he was still trying to get home. She looked over the side of the wagon at her new rug. It was beautiful with its churning whirlwinds. The perfect storm.

She pulled the rug off The Last One and walked to the car.

She looked at Rachel. "Tell them The Last One disappeared into the storm we had."

"What storm?" Rachel asked.

"This storm," Shimá said and motioned to the world around them.

Rachel translated and the administrator asked, "Gone where?"

Shimá looked toward the mesa. The sun colluded with her by creating a shadow on her face. "Into the storm."

"Is Claude home?" he asked. The administrator tried to walk past the mules toward the wagon, but they tossed their heads and rattled their reins. The dogs who had been sniffing his and Beatrice's shoes backed away. One's hair lifted on his neck.

"Where is father?" Rachel asked. "Maybe he should talk to them."

She looked at the man. She was taller than the administrator, and she could see that the top of his head was beginning to freckle with age. His eyebrows were long and nearly covered his eyes. "Claude's butchering at his in-laws." She motioned up the road farther. The road went up a steep hill and had ruts a foot deep. "I'm sorry for your trouble." Shimá held the rug out to Beatrice. "For the school."

"It's beautiful." Shimá laid it out on the hood of the car. "Your work is astonishing." Shimá folded it and handed it to her. "It must be hard to let it go."

Rachel translated this to Shimá. She looked away at the hills. "Very hard." Shimá told Rachel to tell Beatrice and the administrator that if Ruth appeared, they'd bring her back like always.

"She was warned—" the administrator began.

"Tell them we must go." Then Shimá spoke to them directly in her language. "We have to gather the last of the pumpkins before the frost tonight." Shimá climbed back into the wagon while Rachel translated for her. Shimá watched her daughter, heard her make a long explanation, and wondered what she was saying. Rachel got back up and sat next to Sarah.

Shimá clicked her tongue and drove the wagon off the road toward the trail that led to the field. The wagon squeaked and the reins jingled. The dogs ran ahead, knowing where they were going. No one breathed. No one spoke. Behind them, the car's engine turned over and over, eventually catching and sputtering to life. Shimá heard the gears grinding, the car turning and going back where it came from.

Shimá stopped the wagon at the top of the hill. She looked down into the wash that was already dark, as if water were running through it. She thought of a story that The Last One had learned at school, from the Black Book. "Shimá," she had said, "there's a story in that book about a woman and her children escaping a city that held nothing but darkness. They say we—you and me and father and everyone that isn't going to church—live in darkness. They told the woman, Lot's wife, she could leave the darkness, but to never look back. 'If you do, you'll turn to a pillar of salt,' they told her. I thought about her when Father took me back to school that first time. I thought, I'd give up my arms and legs and become a pillar of salt to stay here, forever, on this hill. The sheep could come lick me, and you could chip little pieces off of me for the meat. I turned and looked back the whole way, until I couldn't see the sheep or the smoke from your fire anymore." The Last One had pinched her brown arm to show her mother she was still made of flesh and bone.

Shimá clicked her tongue and drove Heaven and Hell toward the field. She knew what was behind them, and she accepted the darkness in front of her.

Once in the wash, where only the old buzzard who flew toward his roost in the south could see them, Rachel and Sarah jumped down and looked in the back of the wagon.

"She *is* gone," Sarah exclaimed.

The Last One, who had curled into a tight ball, opened her eyes and said, "Here I am."

And then the sisters laughed. They were children after all. Children who were hungry, who ate and drank the food Shimá had brought as night covered them and the harvest moon rose over the hills that sparkled. She listened to her children chatter between themselves, sometimes in English. She didn't understand what they were saying much of the time. She didn't care.

The air began to bite with frosty teeth. "We need to get the pumpkins up," she told them.

Sarah stared at the field, counting how many there were. She said they looked like thirty administrators all with bald heads under their hats. She ran into the field, stooped to pick one that barely fit in her arms. When she lifted the pumpkin, a small brown field mouse scurried from under it. The Last One, who had gotten in the wagon and was moving it forward, jumped down like a hawk, caught the mouse, and held it up by its tail in front of her sister's face. Sarah dropped the pumpkin, screamed, and tried to bat it away.

Shimá found two big rocks and approached The Last One. "Hold it still." She meant to smash the squeaking and squirming mouse, but The Last One dropped it. The mouse scampered off across the bright field. Shimá watched it go.

"Tsk," she said. "Next year that mouse and her babies will be back and eat all my pumpkins." She dropped the two stones and turned her broad shoulders to the children. Her face opened into a smile, then closed again as she stooped to pick a pumpkin.

Oh, how she envied that little mouse.

LET THE GOOD TIMES ROLL

You were once a star in the morning sky, that one that hung over the big mulberry in the Anderson's yard at the end of Sierra Drive. You were just hanging around when this comet named Albert came whizzing by and you broke his heart, but in a good way. You pulled him out onto the dance floor and under the Milky Way disco ball, you twirled around and he fell in love and just kept falling until he became a fine layer of dust that blew in your living room again one late afternoon, a summer's day, when hope seemed so far away.

You were once one of those little granules that loves the TV screen like a daytime soap-opera star, but not a star, a comet, part of a tiny whirlwind created over the turntable where you're playing those old records, those songs you used to dance to while your husband was at work.

Now the comet named Albert rises when you get out the duster, and you chase him around the room, twirling in that dress with tiny blue flowers.

But he's always been there. He was in the flour on your hands when you'd pat out fry bread or tortillas, or make sugar and cinnamon donuts for your kids. He was once the dust that today will rise up and be inhaled by you into your lightning-stricken lungs and be blown back out in the form of a kiss.

HELP ME MAKE IT THROUGH THE NIGHT

I guess you both planned it that way, the way he left. I guess it was better than a big fight and him storming out the door with a suitcase, yelling, "You all just keep the house, you bunch'a lazy—" even though us kids didn't know we were Indians. We just thought we were Protestants with a really good tan. And you're yelling back at him in a language foreign to us, as doors slam, dogs growl, and the sky turns the color of a really good Tequila Sunrise. He stomps through the grass that used to be in the front yard and tears off in his truck, careening around the corner. You throw rocks, and the crows call after him, "Yeah, well, we don't need you."

But that wasn't what happened.

Us kids were in the den, huddled around the color TV like wolf pups. It must have been a Friday. *Barnaby Jones* was on. We had a car like Barnaby, except ours was tricked out with an eight-track player and cloth seats. He entered the room with a suitcase the same shade of Barnaby's LTD and set it down, even though he said he was leaving.

With tears in his blue-green eyes, he said it was the hardest thing he'd ever have to do, but he did it anyway. Dad was brave. He left us sitting there on the yellow plaid couch that always made the back of my legs itch in the summer.

It must have been summer.

The TV flickered as Brother and Sister cried openly, shamelessly. I, like a real Indian or Protestant, hid my sorrow outside, where the sky was not magenta, and Dad's pickup, with a camper and rearview mirrors that stuck out like big ears, didn't careen around the corner but turned, rather slowly. Gravel crunched under the wheels, and it sounded just like a line from a good ol' country Western song, just like a line in a story about us, just like that—

And then he was gone.

SUSPICIOUS MINDS

It was said that a long time ago, twins were born. One was named Lightning and the other Thunder. Thunder and Lightning were separated at birth, causing drought and Uncle Tito to lose his four front teeth. One twin was taken across the sacred mountain to the East, over the dry grass of Texas, through Shawnee, Oklahoma, and on into Tennessee. The other twin remained in the shadow of Turtle Mountain in the north valley of Albuquerque. Neither twin knew of the other's existence.

As Lightning grew, he had one unfortunate incarceration after the other—always involving fire. "From an early age," his mama told the judge, "he's had a real knack for burnin' down just about anything."

After seven years in the federal penitentiary, the state of Tennessee released Lightning and asked him never to return. He kissed his sobbing mama goodbye and got on the first Greyhound headed west. They stopped for gas in Memphis at the Conoco gas station where he bought an orange soda, a gold-plated necklace with a lightning bolt and the letters "TCB" above it, and a pair of gold-rimmed sunglasses, and then he returned to the bus. Women looked up demurely from the *National Enquirer*, and men pulled their cowboy hats down over their eyes.

They crossed the hill country of Arkansas and Oklahoma. Lightning watched it pass behind his dark sunglasses, feeling the bolt on his chest shiver with fever. When the bus broke down in Amarillo, they stayed just long enough for Lightning to eat a seventy-two-ounce steak and have his picture taken at the Cadillac Ranch.

Back on the road, the clouds over the dry desert moved ahead of them as they crossed the state line from Texas into New Mexico. Then Lightning jumped out of his seat and stood at the front of the bus, demanding that the driver let him out immediately.

The door wheezed shut and the Greyhound kicked-up dust, heading back out onto the interstate. A passenger with a beehive hairdo looked at a Polaroid picture of Lightning standing beside one of the inverted, half-buried Cadillacs and murmured, "Gawd, he looks just like Elvis." An old woman crocheting an Afghan blanket with black-and-white zig-zags stopped her frenetic needles long enough to make the sign of the cross. The driver looked in his rearview mirrors and saw Lightning on all fours, kissing the ground.

Thunder roared east down I-40 in her cherry 1957 Chevy, a skinny brown elbow stuck out the open window. Her black hair greased back didn't budge an inch as the hot desert wind whipped in around her. Chuck Berry dared her to be good as the fuzzy dice hanging from the rearview mirror rocked back and forth. She plunged over the mountains of Santa Rosa and out across the bone-dry mesa.

Thunder was on her way to a car show and presumably another first-place trophy. She'd give it to her grandmother, who'd put the statue in a curio cabinet alongside her salt-and-pepper shaker collection and an old Hopi kachina doll.

She was nearing the town of Tucumcari, "The Land of the Dinosaurs'" and home of the best green-chile-cheeseburger this side of Turtle Mountain, when she did a double take. On the other side of the road with his thumb pointing west was the King himself.

Thunder turned the huge wheel of the Chevy. Tires squealed and horns blared from oncoming traffic as she bumped across the dirt median and came skidding to a stop on the other side of the interstate. She jumped out and stood beside her car, tailpipes red hot and shaking like metallic rattles. She pulled off her gold-rimmed sunglasses and squinted into the eastern sun. A cloud that had been white as cotton turned dark over the sand hills pocked with meteorite craters and sage-brush. The cloud twisted and shape-shifted from puffy bunny rabbit to squirming serpent or fire-breathing dragon. A tumbleweed the size of a Yugo crossed the interstate heading south.

Thunder and Lightning approached each other: Thunder with her flat chest pushed out and Lightning with his skinny chest sunk in. To the naked eye, in the world of Elvis impersonators and wannabes, it seemed like just another overly nostalgic meeting of minds—driver and hitchhiker headed off to Vegas to try their hands at craps or slots.

But as the Chevy drove off with one skinny elbow out the driver's window and another skinny elbow out the passenger's window, the cloud followed them. As they made the circle off the interstate, droplets of rain kissed the crystal-clear windshield and evaporated off the hood.

Lightning peeled the cellophane off a cassette tape he'd purchased back home, before he'd even left, knowing one day he'd have a ride with some tunes. He handed it to Thunder, and she popped it in the player and cranked up the volume. The familiar "boom" of the bass followed by the "cha-chichi-cha-chichi-cha-" of the high hat. The sound of Thunder and Lightning and the rain hitting the metal roof filled the car and echoed through the canyon of their hearts. The sky cried sheets of rain as the monsoons returned to the Land of Enchantment at last.

(And Uncle Tito's dentures finally arrived from the Veteran's Administration.)

One time the Econoline got stuck in the sand out there at this casino at the edge of the world. We had to carry our gear halfway across the desert. Jeannie J has always had a limp, and while she walked her tambourines and cowbells, her maracas and rattles made a real cool rhythm. I made that the intro drum solo to "Viva Las Vegas." It was its own song, an original. I called it, "We Walk with Our Offering."

—*One Foot*

S

Live at the House at the Edge of the World

Music expresses that which cannot be put into words and that which cannot remain silent.

—*Victor Hugo*

Music is my religion.

—*Jimmy Hendrix*

I do remember the first time she told me how she wanted to disappear. She wanted to be cremated and sprinkled over the Vegas strip. "That's where I want to be," she said. I don't know if the Diné have a name for Vegas. I call it "the place my mom knew like the back of her hand, where there's no time, and it shines like Christmas."

"Over the strip," she said, and we laughed.

I could see myself and, of course, my partner Bubbles, as she nicknamed her, riding shotgun with me in a rented helicopter over the *Bellagio* and *New York, New York*—the miniature Statue of Liberty holding her flame high. Bubbles and I have big-ol' aviator headphones over our ears like the kind Jay-Z would wear in the studio or above the dance floor while he's spinning tunes. The pilot wears a buzz cut and military-style sunglasses even though it's getting dark. He's handsome and capable looking. I yell, "Can I open the window?" and he yells back, "No." I look at Bubbles, and we both know that we aren't wasting this two-hundred-dollar trip. So in a swift move like a cowboy pulling a gun, like an Indian pulling out an arrow to sink into the enemy's heart, like a daughter about to toss her mom out of a helicopter, Bubbles undoes the latch, I push open the window, and she is gone. A cloud of gray ash a thousand feet above the place that she loved the most, even though she never said that. The pilot yells at us as the blades whirl and twist her up and over her place that shimmers. Then he sees me crying and shakes his head. Does he say crazy Indians or crazy lesbians? All I know is that she got what she wanted and she's laughing and laughing, as I cry.

BREATHE (2 AM)

The waitress stops at the booth with a gallon of milk and pours Albert another glass. Refills for all nonalcoholic beverages are free in the coffee shop after 10:00 p.m. The table has a series of white rings on it. With his large, clumsy fingers, he takes several napkins from the dispenser and wipes the table then places his glass on a clean one.

Ruth stirs artificial sweetener into her coffee, observes Albert's shaky hand reaching for the glass, how his lips seek the rim of it, unsure of himself, as if his lips are searching for those of another, a first kiss or maybe a last.

She can't help but think of Albert's dead grandson. He'd raised him after his mother left the boy to Albert and his wife. Then his wife died and they were on their own. But Ruth says nothing of that. Instead, "Have you seen the coyote in the parking lot?"

"A coyote? No, I sure haven't."

Albert's grandson was killed by the police in front of a Circle K when he pulled a knife on his girlfriend then turned it on himself. Ruth kept the front page of the paper with the picture of the young former Marine who'd done three tours of duty in Afghanistan. He had a square jaw like his grandfather's, and, she'd thought, a man with a jaw like that could survive just about anything (and he almost had). But jaws, like most other parts of the body, can lie.

"He was over by the dumpster at the edge of the parking lot. I hope he doesn't have rabies." The coyote had looked at her as it trotted off to the edge of the parking lot, which at 2:00 a.m. on the San Felipe reservation looks like the edge of the world.

"You should get a security guard to walk you out if I'm not here." He'd told her this more than once.

He takes another sip of milk and tries to find the words to tell her he's leaving. She knows this since she'd run into Edith over by the penny slots. Edith, who pushes the refreshment cart around the casino floor, said, "God, I'm going to miss Albert. But who can blame him for leaving?"

Ruth can. Ruth can blame him. She thought of the luxury of it, of giving in to the need to disappear. It was easy for men. They can huddle together anytime, anywhere, but women have to be careful. Albert is someone she'd watched for years before she allowed him to join her for coffee. She knew the slouch of his shoulders, the mint gum he chewed that covered the smell of smoke and beer, the jacket that was not going to impress anyone, the twinkle in his right eye that said there was still some joy left in life. Even if that twinkle, now, is more like a reflection of the machines that sound like a carnival has come to town. He is the last man she will ever really know.

The waitress comes back to ask if there is anything else, and Ruth says yes, she'd like to buy dinner, even though she and Albert have already split a piece of apple pie à la mode. Country fried chicken for her, and the rib eye special for him.

Albert looks at her quizzically. She tells him she hit it big on the Wheel of Fortune machine earlier and had the good sense to move to the penny machines. This is a lie. She lost every bit she came with in the first hour. She'll use her player's card to pay for dinner.

"Edith told me you're leaving," Ruth says, wanting to make something easy for them. "Where to?" She stirs her coffee, takes a sip.

"Florida. My sister broke her hip and needs someone to help her out for a while. I don't think it will be for long. She lives at Dustin Beach. The water is as green as emeralds and the sand white as snow. Maybe you can visit me." He looks away from her and down into his glass of milk.

Ruth sees the pain in his face. She places her hand on top of his, a buoyant touch. Maybe what water from a green sea would feel like if they were both young, and if she was sure. She'd been fooled by herself before, that she was in love with the twinkle in his eye, and not because it reminded her of someone else.

WHERE EAGLES FLY

My mind is very hard to me,
and it's all I carry now.
Your prayers and mine are made of stone,
I can't lift them off the ground.
Your dreams are blurred in sandstorms now, I
carry rock and bone.

What's the matter with you?

LITTLE WING

Simon Begay woke from a nightmare in which he was an eagle. An eagle who had plucked out his feathers and one of his eyes. He held the eye up in a bloody claw and stared at himself curiously. Over the last six months, he'd had variations of this dream. Sometimes, he was soaring, carefree, and then, *bam!* Shot through the eye. Sometimes he only had one wing and could only fly in circles. Regardless, the dreams always ended with blood and feathers scattered around him.

It was 3:00 a.m., and he knew it was useless to try and go back to sleep. He walked to the French doors in his bedroom, pulled back the heavy drapes. Stars twinkled over Hidden Mesa in the cold October morning. Simon's home was in the valley. Sagebrush and rabbit brush were scraggly shadows upon the hills that rolled gradually up toward the mountains to the east and Lonesome Butte to the north. The closest house, his mother-in-law's, was a quarter-mile away. In the moonlight he could make out the outline of it, could see that the light in the kitchen was on. He wondered if his wife was awake too.

Simon plopped down on the bed and rubbed his large head. His wife, Monica, had been staying at her mother, Tahwehweh's, for the last two weeks. She'd left during the Cowboys versus Eagles football game. Just picked up her knitting bag and walked out the door. He hadn't seen or spoken to her since. He'd called the house the next morning. Tahwehweh, who loved Simon, told him to just let her be. "You know how she is."

Yes, that was his fear. He knew how long she could stay mad, like when he'd bought a new truck without consulting her. She didn't speak to him for over a month. She stayed exclusively on her side of the bed. No long arm or leg draped over him. No nothing. And why was she so mad? They had the money. They had his retirement, his consulting fees from the Gaming Commission, his cattle sales. Well, the cattle really were just a break-even deal, but still, he had cash in hand. She had continued sewing new drapes. "Just buy drapes. And trade in your car," he'd told her. But she liked to sew and liked her Ford Taurus. A few weeks later, when she still wasn't talking to him, he tried once again to persuade her, reminding her how well they were doing, how well their children were doing, how well the people of Hidden Mesa *would* do once the casino was built. She looked at him and returned to pounding the beef round they were having for dinner. So, a month after he bought the truck, he took it back to the dealership. The first thing she said when he saw her that evening was, "Where's your new truck?"

Simon exhaled, opened the nightstand drawer, and shook more than the recommended amount of Tums into his hand. He chewed vigorously as he slipped his big feet into bedroom shoes. In the bathroom, he was glad to see in his reflection that he still had two eyes, despite the dark circles beneath them. Cold water on his warm, puffy face felt good. He'd only slept four hours, four fitful hours. It was Sunday, and he'd been asked by a couple of his buddies to go elk hunting. He was certainly up early enough, but he'd already told them he was going to Phoenix to meet with the architect of the casino. He wasn't, because he'd told the architect, who was in Albuquerque, that he was going to Phoenix to see his kids. He wasn't doing that either. He shook several aspirin directly into his mouth.

Well, at least the Eagles had won last night in their playoff game. They'd defeated the Kansas City Chiefs, his grandmother's team.

His grandmother had lived with Monica and Simon the last years of her life. He could still see her wearing her red-and-yellow sweatshirt with a large arrowhead on the front, the letters "KC" embroidered in the center of it. She had become so tiny in old age that her lucky sweatshirt and the recliner chair Simon had bought her swallowed her. She'd lived with them through the lean, losing years of the Chiefs, but no matter how bad they were, her loyalty never wavered. "You never change teams," she'd told him. She found it treacherous that her grandson had been in his lifetime a Denver Bronco, an Oakland Raider, and now a Philadelphia Eagle. "Make up your mind," she'd say in disgust. If she were still alive, she'd have told him with equal disgust to walk himself over to Tahwehweh's house and talk to his wife. "Tsk. What's the matter with you?"

But his grandmother was ten years gone now. Sometimes he felt her boney hand on his forearm, a warm touch. Other times a boney finger poked him in the chest. She'd always told him to think with his heart, not just his head. She had been like a tenacious juniper growing against all odds on a dry hilltop. He, in comparison, felt like a felled tree in a damp forest, decaying. "Go to the medicine man if you're feeling that way," he could hear her say now. But he didn't need a medicine man to know that the hollowness inside him had taken up residence.

Tina Chilli was Simon Begay's grandmother's oldest and dearest friend. She was by far the oldest living member of her clan and quite possibly the oldest living person on the face of the earth. It was said that when she was just a toddler, Tina Chilli, or Teenie as most people called her, crawled like a spider to the top of Hidden Mesa and eventually birthed the entire world from up there. In reality she'd had only one child, a son, who disappeared without a trace four years ago. Every now and then she thought she heard his truck rumbling up the winding road to Hidden Mesa. But a part of him did remain with her, his daughter, Margarita. As Teenie's eyes opened that morning, she remembered the dream she was having about Margarita, who slept in the day bed on the other side of the small house they shared at the top of the world.

"Margarita," she said, in a lilting voice, "I had a dream about you." Teenie had been dreaming a lot lately. She even dreamed while she was awake. Dreams that were like the edges of rain clouds, dreams of eagles and snow. In this dream, Margarita—who was diagnosed at the Albuquerque Indian Hospital when she was a toddler with cerebral palsy and profound intellectual disability, who in this world was confined to a wheelchair with PHS/IHS stamped on the green back rest—could fly.

Teenie smiled and pulled back the Pendleton blanket she'd won at the raffle for Hidden Mesa's girls' basketball team, then her husband's old army blanket, and then the crazy quilt she and her mother had sewn. She sat at the edge of her cot. In the winter she always slept in a stocking cap, long underwear under her cotton nightgown, a black sweater, and her Nike running shoes to keep her feet from swelling. She rocked back and forth, the mattress and her bones creaking, until she had enough momentum to get up. She walked slowly to the woodstove and, holding to the back of a chair, bent down and put little pieces of wood in it. The coals came to life. She filled a blue enamel coffee pot with water and a handful of Folgers coffee.

She hummed a morning song as she opened the front door and peeked out. She clapped her hands together once. "Margarita, it's snowing."

Margarita was awake and smiling, her pillow wet from the spittle that always leaked out of the right side of her mouth. Teenie took the red bandanna that she kept loosely tied around Margarita's neck as if she were a buckaroo, a member of the Howdy Doody Club, and wiped the edges of her mouth. "Good morning, Little Wing," she said to the child.

Margarita writhed in joy, stiffening her spastic limbs even more. She gasped and moaned with delight at the sight of her grandmother.

Teenie repositioned her head so that her face wasn't in the wet spot on the pillow. She whispered to her, "It's time."

Margarita gasped with excitement.

"I'll be right back." She put on her official Dallas Cowboys jacket that weighed nearly as much as she did and pushed open the wooden door. The snow was only about an inch deep, but from on top of the mesa it looked to have covered the whole world, and it was still coming down in flakes the size of communion wafers. She breathed in the sharp air and exhaled laughter.

A narrow dirt road separated the two houses at the top of the mesa, hers and Joe Shorty's. A thin wisp of smoke made its way from the metal pipe on his roof to meet the gray clouds that hovered around them on top of the mesa. They were indeed hidden at the moment. She knocked on Joe Shorty's door. He was nearly as old as Teenie and the last surviving sibling in his family. His wife had passed a long time ago and left him with three daughters. They'd had two sons, also, but both were killed in the Vietnam war before they even had whiskers. He had numerous grandchildren, great-grands, and even great-great grands, as well as nieces and nephews. His children were as numerous as the stars in the night sky and nearly as distant. They came up to the mesa to bring his groceries and wood, but when he asked them to sit down and talk, they scurried out like tiny brown mice.

His family had had a home on the mesa since he was a boy. But there was no running water, no electricity, no WiFi or satellite dishes, so he didn't know who, if anyone, would maintain the home when he was gone. Nobody but the elders wanted to live in such conditions, and due to the fast pace of the world below, there were hardly any elders. Everything and everyone was dying early, including the eagles.

The door to Joe's home creaked open. He emerged from the dark warm house. He had on his winter hat with flaps that covered his large ears and his quilted green-and-yellow lumberjack shirt buttoned all the way to the top. The shirt fell nearly to his permanently bent knees. Joe and Teenie flashed smiles at one another. Joe held a basket in one hand and a prayer stick made of dark feathers, greasy with age, in the other hand. His eyes were like specks of coal that sparked within folds of brown wrinkles. He and Teenie walked back to get Margarita.

Simon had been elected president of the Hidden Mesa Chapter House in a landslide victory: 89 to 13 three years earlier. He had run nearly uncontested until old Dwayne Slim wrote himself in a month before the election. Slim, with the help of Teenie Chilli, made flyers and ran on the platform of voting against the casino, and with the promise that every chapter member would receive a free turkey *and* ham on Thanksgiving *and* Christmas.

Simon's platform was just as simple: increased autonomy by bringing jobs and infrastructure to not only the people of Hidden Mesa but the entire tribe. The casino would be a Class II casino with two hundred slot machines and bingo from which the people of Hidden Mesa would receive 5 to 10 percent of the profits for ten years. During the only debate, Dwayne Slim called Simon's plans for "a glorified Quonset hut" a losing proposition and went on to talk about his time in the military, coming back around to the fact that his barracks were a Quonset hut, and why would they want one sitting on top of Lonesome Butte? Simon's rebuttal, as if one were needed, was that it was prudent to start small and grow. He'd looked out at the crowd of about fifty people, the twelve elders and Margarita included. "My vision for Soaring Eagle is that it will eventually be not only a casino, but a resort destination." Even Monica had giggled over that. The fact was that the casino would have limited access. It was off a highway, not the interstate. "My concern," Dwayne said, "is that the majority of players will be the people of Hidden Mesa and the surrounding districts." Simon's rebuttal was that the population of their chapter was dwindling. "Economic development is the only way to provide the young people an opportunity to stay on their sovereign lands."

Ultimately, the people of Hidden Mesa put their hopes in Simon's vision and voted him in. Two years later, they voted to have the casino built in their district. As a result, Simon gained the respect of the Gaming Commission, the Tribal Council, and most members of his chapter, but not the elders. They remained adamantly opposed to the casino. As a last-ditch effort to stop construction, they had called for a Special Session. That meeting had lasted three hours and only the twelve elders, most on walkers or canes, and Margarita were in attendance. One-by-one they stood, walked slowly to the front of the room, and requested to have the casino plans thrown out. Simon told the Grandmothers and Grandfathers that they had petitioned the same thing last year and it was voted down, unanimously. Stony-eyed, the elders shoved another of their petitions at him and insisted it be taken to the Tribal Council. That petition was still in the glove box of his truck.

Simon was now sitting in his idling truck, on the pretense of looking for his cattle, when actually his binoculars were trained on his mother-in-law's house down in the valley. He was up in the hills where it was snowing already.

Smoke curled out of the stove pipe on her roof. He tried to see in the windows, but the gauzy drapes blurred his view. Even though he didn't see anyone, he could practically smell bacon frying and taste warm tortillas already piled high on a plate, shiny with butter. Monica made the best bread. The proof of that was the belly Simon carried around.

He should just go over, he told himself. Take them some wood. Tahwehweh would let him in. He tried to convince himself that he didn't even know why his wife had gotten so angry. But he did know. He'd acted—been acting—like an asshole. Prior to her leaving, Monica had suggested they go to their time share in Florida, or to Phoenix to visit the kids. He was too busy, he'd said. Yes, yes, the casino, she'd replied. I know.

The way she'd said it stayed with him. It reminded him of the way the elders belittled him. So when he came home after the Special Session, he was not only angry at the elders but angry with her, too. He'd gone immediately to the liquor cabinet. And before she even asked, he told her exactly how the meeting had gone, rambling on and on. ". . . Then," Simon gesticulated, sloshing some of his drink on the carpet, "after three hours—*three hours*," he repeated, "Dwayne Slim literally corners me with his walker." Simon had demonstrated the way that Dwayne had pushed up against him, cornering him, all four foot eight of him. "Tells me that he knows I'm powerless to stop the construction of the casino. Just a pawn. A powerless pawn! The casino was voted on, and I'm acting on the power that came with that vote." Simon finished his drink. "He says he just doesn't have the heart to tell Teenie and the others that the fight is over." Simon thumped his chest, "Like I don't have a heart." Simon shoved the petition to change the name of the casino at Monica. "They think using the eagle in the name of the casino is irreverent."

Monica read the suggestions for alternative names on the petition.

"Jumping Jackrabbit, Laughing Lizard, Rabid Rabbit, Crazy Coyote." She laughed.

Simon snatched the petition back from her. "They're making a mockery of my position." She'd rolled her eyes at him and got up to go to the other room. He followed after her. "They act like I'm getting something out of this."

"Aren't you?"

"I get fees for consulting."

"And trips to Vegas, rounds of golf in Phoenix and Tucson. A new truck?"

"I bought that truck with my money." Granted it was a "bonus" for successfully lobbying the people of Hidden Mesa for the best spot in their district for the casino, on top of Lonesome Butte where the signage could best be seen from the highway.

He'd taken his drink to the living room to watch the game and pout, even though his team was winning. The only conversation he attempted the rest of that evening was with himself and talking smack to the TV about the opposing team, which happened to be Monica's team, the Cowboys. He called them "Cowgirls" and "Cryboys." He declared that his team had a mascot worthy of a real Indian. Then, when the Eagles went into halftime with a fourteen-point lead, he let out a whoop and charged the refrigerator for another beer. He fell back in his recliner and claimed, louder this time, that he was a real Indian, with the heart and spirit of the eagle, despite what other people thought. "I've always been an eagle."

She didn't even look up from her knitting.

Simon realized he made no sense to her. He barely made sense to himself. He went quiet again until there were two minutes left in the game and the Eagles' quarterback was sacked. Simon slapped his hand on the arm of the chair. "What a stupid play. Stupid. I mean, I could see that from the cheap seats." The Eagles lost, and he called the Cowboys a bunch of rednecks and then told Monica he couldn't believe she was one of *them.*

Simon and Monica had been married since they were nineteen, and in all those years of marriage they had never separated. That night, Monica gathered the blanket she was knitting for their new grandchild, placed it in her knitting bag, and walked to the front door. Simon struggled to get his recliner to an upright position as she put on her winter coat. She turned to him and told him in their native tongue, "What's wrong with you." Not a question, a statement, and a slander on par with ignoring a person altogether. She walked out the door after telling him she'd be back when he got his head out of his ass.

It was two weeks later, and she was still at Tahwehweh's house.

Simon turned the heater in the truck on high as the wind picked up. He took a swig of his coffee and poured a bit more Scotch into it. "There's nothing wrong with me."

He might not have been able to convince Monica of that, but if not for his dreams he might have been able to convince himself. He put his head back and closed his eyes. But then he snapped them back open, afraid to see that he was an eagle, an eagle falling.

The snow clouds and their own breath hovered over Teenie and Joe's heads as they pushed Margarita near the edge of Hidden Mesa. Bundled tightly, she smiled and swayed side to side in her wheelchair as if there were music playing. Teenie pulled Margarita's stocking cap down over her ears. Teenie shivered and saw that Joe had frost hanging from his thin moustache. Teenie was concerned about him. He'd had a heart attack two years ago.

"Are you okay?" she asked. "Do you think you'll be able to sing?" He didn't answer and walked back to his house. The snow was falling so thick, and in such big flakes, that within twenty feet he disappeared from sight.

Teenie brushed snow from Margarita's lap and the armrests of her wheelchair. Teenie held to the chair and closed her eyes against the sting of the wind and waited for his return.

She had forgotten about the old song he was going to sing. They had been sitting in Teenie's house after the Special Session and had come to the realization their petition would fall on deaf ears. "Too little, too late," Joe had said, with a dusting of powdered sugar from a donut around his mouth. "Nothing more we can do but pray."

And pray they did. For four days and four nights, and each had a vision.

Teenie's vision had come to her in Shiprock while she was gassing up her truck after taking Margarita to the clinic there. Inside the Speedway station, she saw the headline of the *Albuquerque Journal*. "Construction of New Bridge Halted." Ancient ruins had been found, and the site would need to be excavated. She smiled to herself and then drove straight back to Hidden Mesa to retrieve a bag that contained something about the size of an adult human skull. She and Margarita set off with the bag, turning off the highway at mile marker ninety-two and onto the old sheep trail that led to the top of Lonesome Butte.

"Teenie," Joe yelled.

Teenie's eyes flashed open, and she came back to the moment. Snow swirled around her and Margarita.

"Here." He handed Teenie a set of wings and placed an old coiled basket in Margarita's lap. Joe took off his lumberjack shirt. His arms were skinny, and his long underwear hung on him. Teenie strapped the wings onto his arms.

Joe's vision had come to him in the form of a song, while he was playing a game of solitaire one night. At first he thought it was just the ringing he sometimes got in his right ear, but, no, it was a song sung very high like the cry of an eagle. It was a song his uncle had taught him as part of the Moccasin Game. "Every animal has a song and a purpose within the game. The eagle song would only be used if a player had no idea what his next move should be. It's a tell, like the way your left eye blinks when you aren't being truthful with your mother." His uncle smiled at him, and then on that cold winter night long ago when Joe was only twelve, his uncle sang the song for Joe. When he finished, he told Joe, "I never had to use it, but one day you might need it."

Today was that day.

Joe had been a pow wow dancer as a young man. He did the hoop dance and the eagle dance. As Teenie tied the wings onto his thin arms, she thought of the way he was back then. Something to behold when he danced. But now he was an old man who'd had a heart attack and was just skin and bone.

"Joe, are you sure?"

"Today's the day."

Teenie stepped back, and Joe began to sing. Slowly he picked one foot up and put it down, then the other. He nearly toppled over just doing that, but then he shot out a wing to balance himself, and gradually she could see his old confidence return.

Teenie stood beside Margarita and listened to the words of the old song not even she or Joe knew the full meaning of anymore. They watched Joe dance. Lowering his body at his hips, bending farther his contracted knees. He danced with arms outstretched, his wings nearly as long as he was tall. But the effort to lift them, the effort to fly did not show in him. He turned slowly, dipping one shoulder, then the other, looking up and looking down. Alternating legs, picking one up then the other, crossing them over each other, squatting so low that his knees nearly touched his chin. He bent so low at one point he looked to Teenie like he might break into two. But he didn't. He danced, light as an eagle, skipping across the snow.

And then a dark feather floated through the thick air like a black snowflake. It landed softly in the basket in Margarita's lap. Its owner, an eagle, followed, landing beside Joe. Teenie and Margarita both gasped. The eagle stretched his wings, and he and Joe danced around one another. Bowing their heads, looking to the sky, stretching their wings, moving in circles. Joe singing a song, bringing it back from the edge of memory, from the edge of time.

Then another feather fell and another eagle landed, and then another, and another, until the basket was filled with feathers and the mesa full of eagle dancers. Margarita rocked in her chair as the song rose and fell, disappearing and returning to earth a little stronger each time.

Joe's voice and his knees never gave out until the last eagle had flown away. Then Joe collapsed like a great bird, like a snow angel, wings out to his sides, eyelashes and nostril hairs covered in frost. His mouth was open like he was trying to catch snowflakes on his tongue, and his eyes didn't move. He seemed to be staring at the black specks soaring out of the quilt of clouds.

Teenie bent over, holding to Margarita's wheelchair. "Joe, get up."

Nothing.

"Joe." She stared at his face, his boney chest to see if she could detect a rise or fall. She uncovered one ear from his stocking cap. "Joe. Joe are you dead?"

He didn't answer.

Joe's eyes moved to her face. He smiled. Teenie helped him to his knees, and he used the handles of the wheelchair to pull himself to his feet.

They pushed Margarita through the snow, laughing, as their tracks and the tracks of the eagles were covered by a great gust of wind.

Simon had driven west to mile marker ninety-two. He'd turned off the blacktop highway onto the old sheep trail and up the gentle rise of Lonesome Butte. On the opposite side of the rise was an abrupt drop. The craggy stones jutted up like teeth, where once upon a time the eagles nested. The last eagle, according to Teenie, was the one that had been found at the bottom of Hidden Mesa. Teenie had brought up the eagle the night of the Special Session as Simon walked her and Margarita out to her truck. "That was the last one that ever visited the old mesa. It's a bad sign, Simon. You know that."

"I'm having the matter investigated. The eagle may have been shot."

Teenie stopped and looked up at Simon. "I didn't read about it in the *Hidden Mesa Newsletter*, along with the 'Turkey Give Away.' Which, by the way, they ran out of turkeys before I got mine." She poked a bony finger up at him. "I'm the one who found the eagle. He wasn't shot. Just dead."

In the dark with her heavy coat pulling her shoulders down and a scarf tied snuggly beneath her chin, she looked like a crow and was just as noisy.

"Things die, Grandmother." Simon called all the elder women "grandmother" out of respect. Simon had stooped down and lifted Margarita out of her chair and placed her in the truck, positioning pillows all around her to keep her from falling over and fastening her seatbelt. "Good night, Margarita." Margarita rocked back and forth and smiled even more broadly at Simon as Teenie slammed her door shut. It had sounded like a gunshot through the valley.

As he reached the top of the butte, he saw among the sagebrush, yucca, and juniper trees the very tops of the yellow flags plunged into the hard earth that denoted the site plan for the casino. Soon they would be covered in snow completely.

He got out and the silence filled him. He sat on the tailgate. *It's a bad sign.* He took a swig from the thermos, devoid of coffee now, just Scotch. It warmed his belly. He looked out and thought about when he was a boy, and the snow made it look like the people of Hidden Mesa were the first and only people, or like in his comic books, lone survivors of the planet.

The power lines for the casino would follow the old sheep trail to the top of the butte. He'd been assured by the Tribal Council that the lines would go beyond the butte to the homes farther out that didn't have electricity. Assured that the high-speed internet at the casino and its associated tower would allow for greater access of that service for the people. "Promises," Teenie had said, and laughed at him. "Just like they promised Dwayne that he'd have power and water to his house when they rolled that government house out there. They could have at least left the wheels."

The infrastructure alone was worth the turmoil it had raised among the members of the district and tribe. He heard his wife's advice to him months ago, "Pray about it. And don't let your heart get as hard as your head." He had prayed, and all he received in return were nightmares.

He slid off the tailgate. He needed to go look for his cattle in earnest. He got his binoculars and walked to the edge of the butte. His foot slid into a hole and he fell. He rolled to his side, laughing at himself. As he got to his knees, he saw that there was something in the hole. He dug out a pot. A full-size pot, a canteen, not even cracked. He turned it over, and something hard rumbled inside of it. He shook it but nothing came out.

He'd never found anything like it. There were shards of pottery all over the hills, in the valley, all around the reservation. The shards were considered to be ancestors and were not to be moved. They were so common that finding shards didn't warrant halting construction. But a whole pot? He examined it closely. The color and design suggested rain clouds had opened above a mountain. There was a feather design arching like a rainbow above the tall mountain. Remarkable, he thought. It reminded him of a pot his grandmother had. The pot she had given to her best friend, Tina Chilli.

Teenie.

"I'm takin' this to the Supreme Court, Simon," she'd yelled over the furious pumping of her foot on the gas pedal and the turning over and over of the engine of her truck after the Special Session.

"On what grounds, Grandmother?" Simon yelled over the truck that found a spark and roared to life with a belch of smoke.

"On the grounds you're building a casino on sacred ground. Our ancestors' spirits will be disturbed. You know that." She revved the engine. "Think about your grandmother."

He looked at the pot. "The land holds memory. Learn from it," she'd told him. All around him was his grandmother's world, his world too, and it required a healthy sovereign nation to maintain it and the people. Soon the elders at Hidden Mesa would be gone, and he would be an elder, the one people looked to for answers.

He looked at the pot. "I'm sorry, Grandmother. It's already done." He lifted the pot above his head and meant to smash it when the object inside fell out. A US half-dollar glistened upon the snow. The eagle on it looked as if it were landing or taking flight. Its wings were spread out to its side, and its head was turned so that it looked like it only had one eye.

It screamed, or he heard screaming. He wheeled around, wondering if he were in a nightmare. Then an eagle shot past his head, its wings grazing him, nearly knocking his Philadelphia Eagles cap off. He watched it arch up, flap its great wings, and head east toward the mesa. He blinked. He must be in a dream, he saw eagles, too many to count flying toward the mesa. He looked through his binoculars. Something flashed, snow lightning, or something metallic falling from the mesa to the base below. He thought of something Teenie had told him that night in the parking lot. "Margarita's learning to fly."

He saw blood and feathers and crushed metal at the bottom of the mesa. He got in his truck and raced toward Hidden Mesa.

Teenie and Joe were waiting inside when they heard a truck rumbling up the road. Teenie put on a pot of water for coffee. But then they heard nothing except crushing metal.

Now they peered over the edge of the mesa at the truck laying on its side, wheels still spinning. They saw Simon, trying to pull himself out the window.

"Simon," Teenie yelled. "Are you okay?"

"We can throw you a rope," Joe yelled.

Simon fell onto the ground with a cry of pain, then got up, and like a rabid three-legged dog began to climb out of the ravine. Through short gasps for breath he yelled, "Did you see them? The eagles?"

"What?"

Simon, holding his arm at his side, managed to get to the road, then fell onto his back gasping for breath. Teenie could see that blood covered one whole side of his face. He pointed up with his good arm. Teenie looked up at the eagles soaring toward what looked like a hole in the sky. He got back up and started trying to run up the road. He'd fall and grunt and then get back up again, muttering and gasping and grunting until he got to the top. He had sweat pouring down his face. Droplets of blood trailed behind him as he ran past Teenie and Joe.

He reached out toward the sky. "No, don't go." He fell to his knees.

Teenie stood beside him. "Simon. What's the matter with you? You know better. That road in the snow—your truck is ruined, and you could have been killed. Tsk."

"Grandmother, did you see them? You must have seen them. They were landing up here."

She touched his head. "You got a big knot and a broken wing."

"Where's Margarita. What have you done with her?"

The inside of Teenie's house smelled just like his grandmother's, sweet and dusty. He looked around and saw her, his grandmother, sitting in her old wheelchair. The eye that wasn't sealed shut teared. He smiled and got closer to her. But where was Margarita? He whirled around and stumbled.

"Simon. Sit down!"

Joe slammed the door to the wood-burning stove shut and poured himself a cup of coffee. Simon fell into the little chair at the table.

Teenie placed a warm towel on Simon's eye. She shook her head. "You know, your grandmother, my dear friend, she thought you were the best thing since fry bread. She would tell me, 'Someday, Teenie, someday he'll be a great leader. You'll see. One day he'll fly.' I don't think she meant off the mesa in your truck though." She gently wiped the caked blood from his eye and looked into his other one.

He took her thin hand and held it. "Did you see them?"

Teenie smiled at him. "Of course I did. How could we have missed them."

"Thank God. I thought it was one of my—but it was real. It's a good sign." He let go of her hand, exhaled, and touched the knot on his forehead. He was suddenly happy, happier than he'd felt in some time. As if all his concerns had been lifted. He needed to talk to Monica. Wanted to hold her, wanted her to hold him. He looked again in the corner at the wheelchair and saw that of course that wasn't his grandmother, it was Margarita. Of course. He laughed. "It's a good sign."

Margarita moved her head side to side. Teenie retrieved the basket in Margarita's lap and showed Simon all the eagle feathers. "I'm glad you can see that. I'm glad you've come to your senses." She patted him on the shoulder.

"What do you mean? 'Come to my senses.' I prayed, and the eagles blessed the decision I made, that we made, that we voted on."

She took the bowl of warm water, tinged with Simon's blood from the table.

Joe sat down with a plate of donuts. "You weren't the only one praying, Simon." He held a powdered donut out to him.

"The eagles have blessed her. Look! Look at all the feathers they left."

"Margarita?" He laughed. "She can't even—she's—"

"Nonverbal," Teenie said. "But you, Mr. Big Talker, you think you're the one with the heart to lead us. The eagles think otherwise." Teenie turned her back to him and put more wood in the stove.

"If I'd gotten here sooner—but you gathered them all up for yourselves."

"You ran your truck off the road trying to get here. Don't you think that's a sign, too?"

Joe said, "Every time I've gotten into a car wreck, and I've had six, it was a sign. The first one, I was only twenty-one, going on a blind date. I—"

Simon got up quickly, too quickly. He wavered, and the chair crashed to the floor. "You're playing tricks on me. You planted that pot at the construction site. You knew I'd find it." He laughed. "Do you think I'm that stupid? I see what you're doing." His head pounded. "You're pulling out all the stops, the three of you, but it won't work. You disrespect my authority—and you gift her, who can't even take care of herself, who can't even walk, with the blessings that were mine."

"Don't act like a child. Sit down and think about it for a minute. The blessings are all of ours. You aren't the only one who has visions, or nightmares in your case."

"How do you know that? Monica," he said, exasperated. "Talking behind my back."

Teenie shook her head. "Worried about you. She told me to talk to you, give you my blessing on this so that you could sleep again. But your sleep, your peace of mind, is in your own hands. All we ask now is that you find another spot for the casino. Closer to the chapter house, or—"

But he couldn't. It was the deal he'd made to get the casino in their district.

"No." He wobbled to the front door and fell against it. His head was spinning, but he was determined to show them that he too had received a blessing from the Creator. "I'll find a feather," he said, sneering at her.

Outside the clouds were gone, and the sun reflected off the snow so brightly his head felt like it was cracking in two. "I know they left one for me," he muttered.

Teenie and Joe followed him, pushing Margarita to the door. They watched him walking through the snow, falling down and getting back up.

"Simon," Teenie yelled. "Come away from the edge." She pushed Margarita out of the way to get to him. "Come back."

Margarita arched in her chair, the basket tilted, and the feathers spilled out, but instead of landing they floated above her.

Simon turned and saw the feathers. He blinked. Margarita was gone, and in her place was an eagle, talons wrapped around the armrest of the wheelchair. It screamed.

He walked toward it, and then it was Margarita again, a big smile on her face. She squealed with delight as the feathers began to move all around him, like he was the center of a whirlwind. He spun, wincing in pain, chest pounding, and within that pounding he heard a song. A familiar voice, happy and sad at the same time. His grandmother. Singing an old song about a child who could fly.

"Do you hear that?" His face broke into a smile. "Shhh," he put his fingers to his lips. "Listen."

He turned in circles, looking for the singer, looking for his grandmother. Sweat dampened his clothes, and it must have been that dampness, he thought, that made the feathers begin to stick to him. He stopped and saw that his arms were covered in feathers. Wings. He had wings.

"Do you hear that?" He looked up at the sky. Then he realized it was him. Him screaming, him singing. His voice rose and fell. The dance drew him closer and closer to the edge of the mesa. Until there was no edge, only sky. There was no sound, except the cry, the song, the prayer of an eagle.

"I hear it," Teenie yelled after him as she watched, not a man falling to the ground, but an eagle taking flight and soaring, up and up, until he was only a black speck in a clear-blue sky.

ALBUQUERQUE JOURNAL, NOVEMBER 21, 2011

TRIBAL POLICE HAVE not ruled out fowl play in the disappearance of the chapter president of Hidden Mesa, Simon Begay. Two elder members of the district, Tina Chilli and Joe Shorty, were the last to see Begay on Tuesday morning. Also present was Margarita Chilli, who is nonverbal, but made it clear by moving her arms out to her sides like wings, that she agreed with her grandmother, Tina Chilli, when she stated, "Simon turned into an eagle and flew off the top of the mesa." Mr. Begay's truck was found in a ravine off the road to Hidden Mesa. Bloodstains were found in the truck. The keys were still in the ignition, and an empty thermos was found on the floorboard. His wife was interviewed and stated she had not seen Begay for two weeks, when she left to stay with her mother, Tahwehweh Manyhorses, because Mr. Begay "was acting like an idiot." When questioned as to whether he was violent, she said, "No, he was just very annoying. Something was the matter with him." Mrs. Begay reports that she did not see him that morning, but woke to hear an eagle crying. "When I went outside there was snow everywhere and an eagle feather laying outside the front door of my mother's home." When told what Tina Chilli had said, Mrs. Begay looked up to the sky and said, "He was saying just the other night that he'd always been an eagle."

A long time ago, my auntie told me don't let them know you're Navajo. Who are they, and why, I should have asked, but I didn't. I knew why, or at least why she thought it was a good idea to hide. But more than that, I didn't want anyone to know I was a lesbian. So, I disappeared. Finally, one day, I looked in the smoky mirror and saw Jeannie J, lead singer for the Covers. I'd sung my way into finding her. These songs are my prayer. "Restore my heart and body to me."

—*Jeannie J*

Live at the House of Red Clay

The great thing about rock and roll is that someone like me can be a star.

—*Elton John*

. . . rarely, if ever, are any of us healed in isolation. Healing is an act of communion.

—*bell hooks*

CHILDREN OF THE SUN

walk straight into bright light, like one of those children of the sun on the cover of *Houses of the Holy*, except I'm not naked on the steps of a pyramid. I wear Ray-Ban sunglasses and SPF-50 to shield me from the sacred, to protect me from the free radicals that have formed already and are surging through my blood stream, erupting onto the not-so-young-and-tender skin of my forearms, freckles that are trying to speak to me of death in the only language they know—the language of stars.

They tattoo my arms with constellations so that I will need: a PhD in astronomy, an astrologer with long red nails, a map of the night sky, the Hubble Telescope, the VLA, a scientist with eyes like Jodie Foster, someone as lonely as I am to understand the galaxy I have become, the silence between stars, death without dying.

PERSONAL JESUS

When I was little, I used to take holding on to things literally. For instance, I fell in love with my neighbor Missy. Missy resembled Cindy Brady from the *Brady Bunch*. One afternoon, after watching *Dark Shadows* at Missy's house, we went to play in Missy's bedroom. Missy had a tiny bowling set complete with a miniature bowling ball that she kept on her dresser. I loved the little set nearly as much as I loved Missy, but even at the young age of six, I knew this love may not be returned. So, I took a memento, one of the pins. What better way to keep Missy next to my heart then in a cigar box beneath my bed?

That's why small things that might be missed, but couldn't be found, began to disappear around our house. Like my sister's troll doll, a tube of lipstick from my mom's purse, a belt buckle I "found" in my dad's top drawer. It must have been from when he was in the navy, because it had a mermaid and an anchor on it.

My fear was that catastrophe could strike at any time: fire in the middle of the night burning up the house and my family, a car accident while my parents were driving home from eating out, a punctured lung if someone fell off their bike wrong, drowning, kidnapping, someone running away and leaving me behind.

I was pretty sure that if the good Lord showed up in the middle of the night, or on a sunny afternoon, it would not be with cherubim and seraphim riding noisily into our lives, but more like how my second-cousin Avis arrived—unannounced. But unlike Cousin Avis, who was very visible, who required a kiss on her stubbly chin and assistance in pulling her oxygen tank in the house, God would come in undetected and ride away with a soul.

Vigilance was required. I prayed and I held.

Some nights—for effect only—I would kneel in front of my twin bed, hands squeezed together, gazing up at the popcorn ceiling that had tiny specks of glitter embedded in it. I strived to look pious, like the little girl I'd seen on a Christmas card. Except I wasn't blonde or cute (like Missy), and I didn't have a Christmas tree in my bedroom.

"Now I lay me down to sleep, I pray the Lord my soul to keep . . ."

If I couldn't have Missy, if God took her away, which he did in the second grade to Texas, I had the tiny bowling pin. Or, if a school bus drove over our beagle, I had her new chew toy. And my dad's belt buckle? Call me telepathic. I wondered if he missed it as much as I missed him.

". . . and if I should die before I wake, I pray the Lord my soul to take."

I think he did, a little bit at a time.

INTO THE MYSTIC

I was fifteen. Gloria Gaynor had proclaimed in her classic disco song that she would survive, and so, it turned out, would I. On that day, though, my burning shame had sent me running to my cave.

The Twin War Gods found me there.

The Twin War Gods are both gorgeous. The one who looks more like a girl is called Sitsi. She has long black hair that blows around her. Her power is the wind. The other one that looks more like a boy is called Shiyaazh. He has long black hair that flows straight down over his broad shoulders. His power is the flowing water. They came in that day, long ago—in 1978, back when there was still a glacier on Blue Bead Mountain and gas was eighty-nine cents a gallon.

The twins were breathless as they burst into my cave and looked around, their eyes hidden behind mirrored sunglasses. My cave was freshly mopped, and the pungent, sickening smell of Pine-sol still hung in the air. "Ya'at'eeh," they said in unison and closed the door.

"What are you doing in here?" Sitsi asked.

"Hiding," I replied.

"From whom? Is the cavalry coming?" Shiyaazh asked and pulled out a long sword made of black steel with quartz crystal in the cross guard. Sitsi pulled out a long staff made of hard polished wood with a piece of sharpened obsidian at the tip.

"No, I'm hiding from my mom," I said.

"Oh, so are we." They put their weapons back in the scabbards tied to their narrow hips and looked about my small cave some more. Sitsi rubbed her hand along the smooth Sheetrock above the clothes hamper and knocked on the wall with her knuckles. Shiyaazh ran his brown fingers along the rim of the almond-colored bathtub.

"This is a nice cave," they said in unison, and they began to make themselves at home. They pushed their long black capes over their broad shoulders, and Shiyaazh lay down in the bathtub. "It's nice and cool in here. No wonder you like it so much."

The front bathroom was the coolest place in our ranch-style house. My family had entered a personal drought about two years before, so while the rest of the neighborhood was beginning to turn green, sprinklers making their soft and dreamy *whoosh-whoosh* semicircles around their lawns, our grass, like my father, wouldn't be returning that summer. The little pine tree my mom dug up on the way back from my grandfather's funeral had turned brown and the needles were falling off. The rose bushes already had mites, and both swamp coolers were broken because we didn't know we were supposed to drain them and they'd frozen over the winter. We all missed the clank and clatter they made, the musty smell of desert air conditioning wafting through the house.

Sitsi sat down on the Formica countertop between the double sinks, looked at her reflection, and tried to smooth her hair down. "This reminds me of the lake on top of Mirror Mountain where your great-grandmother had a cave."

I was seated on the only chair in this cave, the toilet with the lid down. "My great-grandmother?"

"You know, the one we call The One That Got Away," Shiyaazh said.

"From the US Calvary?" Sitsi said, raising her eyebrows and then bringing them together above her nose. "She was a great woman. You've never heard of her?"

I shook my head.

Unlike my father's side of the family, whose history is as long and winded as the plains of the Midwest, my mom's family history is like a sand painting that has been destroyed. It would take me years of sneaking around to find newspaper clippings, photos in books and museums, of learning how to listen to silence and remembering low and muttered conversations before I could begin to piece us together.

"I've never heard of her."

Shiyaazh pulled toilet paper from the holder and held a piece out to me. "This story always makes us cry."

Sitsi continued. "She had to run away from her family. She was the only one of the children big enough to possibly get away. So her mother, with tears in her eyes, said, 'Run and don't look back.' And she did. She ran and ran like a rabbit, her fear helping her to leap over bushes and letting her heart race without seizing up. She made it to the place her mother had shown her years before when they were out gathering herbs."

"Oh, what I wouldn't give for a cup of her tea," Shiyaazh said, and sighed.

"Tsk." Sitsi shook her head at her brother and said something in Diné to him and continued with the story. Her voice sounded like a warm summer breeze as it flows across the mesa. "By the time she got to the cave it was already dark outside and even darker inside. The wind was howling nearly as loudly as the wolves outside the entrance. She was cold and hungry. In the quiet of the night she cried for her mother and father, her sisters and brothers. But they had all been captured by the soldiers and were headed to the Place of Sorrow."

They both took off their dark sunglasses and wiped their eyes. Shiyaazh blew his nose loudly, and it sounded like a goose.

"That cave, like this one, had a spring," he said and turned the faucet of the bathtub, filled his hands with water, and rinsed his face. He drank a handful of water. "Ay."

Sitsi continued, "She stayed in that cave for four days and four nights with nothing to eat except dirt. When she emerged from the cave on the fifth morning, even though her mother had told her not to, she looked back from where she had come. She saw the long trail of her people heading away from her and beyond Blue Bead Mountain. She howled like one of those wolves that she'd been hearing every night. That's why some of them called her Mą'ii-tso-bah or Big Coyote Warrior.

"She stayed in that canyon area, afraid to venture out, for four weeks. Then, when she thought that it was safe, she packed up her belongings and decided to head the opposite direction her family had gone. She walked toward the setting sun. They say that the sun would have burned her eyes up if it weren't for all the tears she cried." Sitsi blew her nose, and it sounded like another goose.

Shiyaazh continued, "She learned to hunt and cook rabbits. That's why some called her Gah-tsoh-bah, because she became like a rabbit, turning her fear into power as she walked west to the place that she had heard of years ago from her grandmother. A place called, in the bilagáana's language, Mirror Mountain. And inside of it was another cave. At the top of the mountain was a small lake, and it was there that she learned the fate of her family in its reflection. She saw her family dying in the Place of Sorrow.

I blew my nose, and it sounded like a bugle.

"Then one evening, she was humming a song about love and all its forms when your great-grandfather arrived all shot up. He had a bullet in his left leg, a bullet in his right arm, a bullet in his other leg, and a bullet in his other arm. He was nearly dead."

"But still, he was so handsome," Sitsi said. "He looked like me."

"And, she was so beautiful," Shiyaazh said. "She looked like me."

They both sighed. "And of course they fell in love immediately."

"Your great-grandmother, who knew everything about everything, found just the right herbs. She chewed them up and placed them like kisses on his wounds."

"She was *so* cool," Sitsi said. "She dragged him to the very back of her cave and stayed with him for forty days and forty nights, making sure he was safe and warm and drinking plenty of tea."

"Oh, what I wouldn't give for a cup of her tea," Shiyaazh said.

"And while he healed, she thought about all the children they would have when he got well. You see, she had dreamed of him long before he came bleeding and limping up to her. She was not primitive, as the US government thought. She had her dreams. They thought they owned everything, even our dreams. Ugh!"

The Twin War Gods took their sunglasses off and breathed on them and wiped the lenses with their capes. "She also dreamed of a cave like this, bright and clean."

Sitsi picked up my eyelash curler. "What's this?"

I took it from her and showed her. I opened my eyes wide and scrunched my upper eyelashes in its metal jaws.

"That looks painful," she said.

I did my other one. "So they got married?" I asked.

They nodded and said in unison, "Of course they did. And we wish we could say that they lived happily ever after, but you know in all of our stories nobody lives happily ever after." They both laughed, and when they did it sounded like wind blowing through the dried leaves of a cottonwood tree or the sound of water flowing over rocks in a creek that was clear and bright in the sunshine. "We can't just live, we always have to be learning something."

"What did she learn?"

"She learned how to endure, how to love again even when love has been taken from you, killed, marched across the desert to rot—"

"Okay, okay, take it easy," Shiyaazh told his sister. "I think she gets it. But we're not certain exactly what happened to them. They disappeared, and there aren't any records of them. But they lived long enough to have many children. And those children had children, who had children, and here one sits in a cave—hiding. And, and—it's not fair," Shiyaazh said, and he began to cry and it was as loud as Niagara Falls.

Sitsi got up and put her brother's head on her shoulder. She shook her head and said, "It's not fair."

"What's not fair?"

"That everyone else gets to marry who they want and have children and more children. They're like spiders, they get to have about a hundred children every other day," Sitsi said. "And then there's us."

"Us?"

Big tears plopped down on her black leather pants and slid into the top of her black moccasins that had obsidian buttons up the sides.

"Tell her," Sitsi said.

Shiyaazh shook his head and said, "No, you tell her."

"You see, why we're here, hiding with you, is our mother found out that he's gay," Sitsi said, pointing with her lips at her brother, who had laid back down in the tub and had his eyes covered with his forearm.

"And our mother found out that she," he said, pointing at his sister with his lips, "is a lesbian."

They said in unison, "She's not at all happy."

"How did she find out?"

"She caught me in my cave with my girlfriend," Sitsi said.

"And she found me in my cave with my boyfriend," Shiyaazh said.

"My mom caught me with my girlfriend," I said.

"Where?" the twins asked in unison.

"Um—in my car."

"Your chidi," Sitsi said.

"It's a Ford Pinto," I said. "Midnight blue."

"How nomadic," Shiyaazh said.

"Where were you, the Drive-In?"

"No, we were up on the mesa. It was midnight. I made a fire from little pieces of juniper, sage, and tumbleweeds, and we kissed and kissed. The sparks from the fire twirled up and mingled with the night sky. We made a whole new constellation that night."

"How did your mom find you on top of the mesa?"

"She had a telescope," I said.

The twins wrinkled their faces like newborns.

"Okay, that's a lie. Really, we were in my bedroom on the floor. I have scoliosis, so I'm always more comfortable lying on the floor—or in the bathtub. I read most of *Jaws* in there."

"It's very comfortable," Shiyaazh said, crossing his long legs and placing his moccasined feet up on the cool tiled wall.

"So we were on the floor watching TV. I had been trying to find the perfect time to kiss her, and it just so happened that the perfect time came during *The Brady Bunch*. Alice had just left the house to go see her boyfriend, Sam the butcher, and that's when I made my move. I'd been thinking about that kiss ever since I'd seen James Bond make the same move in *The Spy Who Loved Me*. And boy was it a good one, smooth. And then Alice came home and she yelled, 'Time for dinner. Sam sent us pork chops.'"

"I love pork chops," Shiyaazh said.

"Your girlfriend's a spy?" Sitsi said.

I shook my head. "No, she works at Burger King."

The twins scrunched their faces up again.

"Okay, that's a lie, too. We weren't in my bedroom and it wasn't midnight. There were no stars or pork chops. It was morning, this morning, and I thought my mom had left for work."

My mom, a recently divorced nurse who didn't drink or smoke, who didn't run around or bring strange guys home with her, who was just trying to survive a broken heart, worked at the Indian Hospital.

Before she left for work, I'd told her about my senior research project on black-market babies, which was the topic of the *Phil Donahue Show* that morning, and that my English teacher said it was fine if I came in late. The truth was I only went to school as much as was required to play sports and graduate.

"My friend Doreen—"

"Your girlfriend?" Sitsi asked.

"Yeah, right." I'd been so happy to see her. So in love with her and the freckle on the end of her nose, the way her hair smelled like a place that I thought I would have to be torn away from to ever leave. "She came over when I'd thought Mom had left for work."

"Mothers are sneaky," Shiyaazh said.

"We were just watching *Donahue*—except that Doreen was sitting on my lap and had her arms around me." And we had our tops off, sitting there in the big recliner chair in our crappy bras, kissing, when Mom walked in the door.

"Oh boy," Sitsi said.

"I tried to get up, but Doreen couldn't move. I was pushing and shoving and trying to stand, but she was in shock and couldn't budge."

"If I got caught kissing my girlfriend in front of a nurse from the Indian Hospital I'd be frozen like a wooly mammoth, too," Sitsi said.

"Eh-yah," Shiyaazh said.

My mom just stood there staring at us. I couldn't see her eyes behind her polarized glasses, but I knew what she was thinking. I'd like to lie now and say I did something heroic or brave, but in truth, I began right then to figure out how I was going to get out of this, how I could keep her from hating me. I told her I'd never do it again, and I didn't kiss another woman for ten years. I'd tell counselors later I was trying to keep my family from being hurt, but that's bullshit. I was trying to keep me safe, to keep from having people stare at me like she stared at me that morning.

"Did you say anything to her?" Shiyaazh asked.

"I think I said, 'We're watching *Donahue.*'"

"What else could you say in such a compromised position?"

"No matter what you said, it wouldn't have mattered. We tried to explain to our mom. We told her that we are still the Monster Slayers that we've always been. So what if I feel in love with Fire—she's so beautiful, who wouldn't?" Sitsi said.

"And I fell in love with Ocean—he's so gorgeous, who couldn't?" Shiyaazh said.

"Our mother asked, 'Why couldn't it be the other way around? Sitsi, you fall in love with Ocean, and Shiyaazh, you fall in love with Fire.' We told her if it was that way, then I would eventually flood the world," Sitsi said.

"And I would eventually put out all our fires," Shiyaazh said.

"We reminded her of the powerful Nadleeh—the half-man, half-woman from the old times. She said these were not the old times. That we don't live in the past."

"And she's right. The missionaries changed the way the people thought about Nadleeh."

"'The people will see you as weak and powerless,' she told us. Our mom narrowed her already squinty eyes at us and said, 'Shame on you!'"

They both started to cry. The bathtub began to fill with Shiyaazh's tears and the light bulb above Sitsi's head blew out.

"She banished us from the Dinétah," they wailed. "We can't go back."

I wailed with them, because that's what my mom said before she turned and walked out the door. "My mom told me, 'Shame on you. You kook.'"

"Kook? What's a kook?"

"It's a crazy person—a freak!"

Then Sitsi stood up and said, "Well, I'm not a kook. And neither are you." Her hair flew around her head, and she nearly became a tornado.

Shiyaazh stood up, dripping wet from all his tears. "I'm not a kook either. And neither are you." His hair hung straight down and looked like black sheets of rain.

"Say it, 'I'm not a kook.' Say it, or we may have to kill you."

Then we all heard the front door open and close. "My mom's home," I whispered, and the Twin War Gods jumped into the tub and closed the shower curtain. I waited in my cave for what seemed like four days and four nights until my mom finally knocked on the door and came in. She stood over me in her nurse's scrubs. Her lipstick had worn off hours ago, and her mouth remained set in that beautiful and cruel way.

"I cleaned the house," I told her.

Before the twins had arrived, I had dusted every piece of furniture—the piano nobody could play, the coffee table with its collage of *TV Guide*, the *National Enquirer*, and the *Albuquerque Journal*. I dusted until Pledge oozed from my pores, getting on my hands and knees at the base of the clawfoot oak table, wiping between the toes of that lion as if it were Jesus himself. I vacuumed and mopped, loaded and unloaded the dishwasher, and hadn't watched any more TV (except for *The Merv Griffin Show*). But still I could tell by her eyes this wouldn't make her love me again.

I heard one of the War Gods sniffle, but luckily my mom didn't hear it.

She just looked down on me and said, "Do you want me to get you counseling?"

I shook my head.

Then she turned away, her soft white nurse's shoes making no noise at all as she walked to the front of my cave and left.

That was the only time we ever spoke about it, if you call that a conversation. The shower curtain parted, and the sister and brother peeked out. "That was her?"

"Uh-huh."

"She's tough," Sitsi said.

"She looks a lot like The One That Got Away," Shiyaazh said.

The twins sat down on the edge of the bathtub and sighed. "Well, it's a good cave. We can stay here—how long?" they asked.

"Until my sister gets home."

"Then where will we go?" they asked, scared, having not been outside the Dinétah their whole lives.

"I don't know." And we all hung our heads and cried very softly, so as not to let our mothers know how weak we had become.

HOTEL CALIFORNIA

She picks the music on the jukebox and goes back to sit at the bar of the hotel. It's early still. The only ones there are her and the bartender, who's her clan brother and former lover—a double taboo. The music floats through slanted light, and she smiles at the joy a quarter can still buy in this world.

She pulls her huge sunglasses down and looks over the top of them, winking. "Hey, Junior, can I get a light?" she asks, even though she doesn't smoke.

"Take off those stupid sunglasses," he tells her as he rubs the inside of a glass with his white towel and places it on the shelf above the mirror so the lights and the heat from the lights almost make it sing like real crystal. She knows he's thinking about killing her.

"You hurt my eyes," she says, and laughs because she likes the sound of it. "You know in the world below, you and I were lovers, together we created not only the monarch butterfly but the flower it drinks from."

"Shut the fuck up, Chuck," he says, and he goes to the other end of the bar as the door opens and a cowboy walks in.

"Jean," she says in a whisper, like the legendary film star Jean Harlow whose picture hangs along with many other stars of a similar era on the second floor of the hotel. "My name's Jean. Nobody would name an Indian Chuck." Really, she knew six guys named Chuck and four of them were Indians.

Jean crosses her legs and pulls her red dress down snuggly across her thin thighs. She absently rubs the scar on her right knee, a scar she got when her horse didn't quite make it over the barbed-wire fence they were trying to jump. She nearly broke her neck, and the horse did break his leg; she watched as her uncle shot it, had to, thought that if she watched something she loved die it might make her more of a man.

"Hey, Junior," she says. "Remember when we lived in the Third World and you bought me that red convertible and we rode out to LA in it? Let's do it again. Let's just go, blow this joint," she says in her best impression of a beautiful but aging movie star.

The bartender hisses at her. "Fucking queer—I'm gonna kill you one day."

"I know," she says, and she begins to collect her things: three more quarters, a coaster that's barely used, and a pack of matches. She looks down the bar at the bartender, who's not her clan brother, who has never been her lover in this world or any other but who probably will kill her. If not him, then someone like him, maybe a Navajo, maybe an Apache, a white man, or a cop—who knows, but someone like him will kill someone like her here in Indian Country, and it's all Indian country.

The door to the bar opens, and a shaft of light gives her new stage direction.

"You know, the next world will be forever twilight," she says to Junior, whose name isn't really Junior. She adjusts her big sunglasses, picks up her duct-taped purse, pulls her dress down below her knees, and says her good-byes in a breathy voice.

DO YOU WANNA DANCE?

Dolores stood beside Ruth in the two-car garage, their polarized trifocals not yet adjusted to the darkness. Dolores wore a sun visor from the 2010 New Mexico Bowl game where the Lobos had lost miserably. Ruth had on her fishing hat with numerous fishing flies dangling from it. She was so tall and skinny she looked like a floor lamp. Above the buzz of the flickering fluorescent shop light that hung from the ceiling there was another buzzing sound.

"What's that smell?" Dolores said, crinkling her nose, but she already had a feeling she knew. Ruth had caught something.

Ruth pointed to the Hefty trash bag lying on the concrete floor. A few large horseflies were buzzing around it, and the smell of wet mud, algae, and a wound that needed a dressing change rose from the green bag.

"Is this why you called me?" Dolores asked. "Tsk." She shook her head. "I knew you were up to something," she added in their native tongue.

She said this because normally Ruth didn't call for Dolores to come over to her house. Usually they went somewhere together—basketball games, the casino. Once in a while Ruth, who had retired several years earlier, would meet Dolores for lunch at the university hospital cafeteria. She was fond of the liver smothered in greasy onions and the peach cobbler.

So, when Ruth had called her around lunchtime that day and asked her to stop by, even though Dolores lived nowhere near Ruth, she knew something was up. When she arrived, Ruth was standing in the doorway to her large ranch-style house. She waved her long, thin arm above her head and left the door open for Dolores to enter. The teakettle whistled and steam filled the yellow sponge-painted kitchen. Ruth had already placed two coffee cups on the orange Formica countertop.

Ruth smiled at her friend and said, "How are you?"

"Fine," Dolores said as she placed a Safeway shopping bag on the counter and pulled out Little Debbie sweet rolls. Ruth got out two plates, and Dolores cut them each a generous portion.

"How was your trip to Bloomfield?"

Dolores's granddaughter played in a summer softball league. Her team had made it once again to the state tournament played near her granddaughter's home in the Four Corners, near Shiprock. Ruth poured water into each cup and held up a box of Christmas Spice tea, even though it was August, and a red container of Folgers instant coffee. Dolores pointed with her lips towards the coffee, and Ruth set it down on the counter beside two spoons.

"We came in second."

Dolores's grandkids always came in second. Second in the girl's 2-AA District basketball tournament, second in the elementary school spelling bee, second in the fancy dance contest, even Dolores had come in second in the quilt show at the county fair. "We got beat by the Bloomfield Sunflowers," a team of freckle-faced farm girls whose team was sponsored by the Future Farmers of America. The Shiprock Screaming Eagles were sponsored by Mo's Transmission Shop and the Chat-N-Chew.

Dolores picked up a spoon and a plate with a frosted sweet roll and followed Ruth to the kitchen table. The sun streamed in the window that faced south, and their trifocals became lightly polarized. The window, wide and low, looked out across what used to be a back lawn, a dirt alley that used to be an irrigation ditch, into Sophie Martinez's yard, and quite nearly into her house. But they could stare into Sophie's house all they wanted, because she was blind. She'd been going blind when Ruth and her family moved into their newly constructed home nearly forty years ago. Now it was Ruth who was going blind. She had been told a couple months ago she had the beginnings of glaucoma. She was keeping it a secret from everyone, including her nosy daughter.

"Is that Junior?" Dolores said, then took a big bite of sweet roll as she looked out the window at a thin man hoeing two rows of corn. Bent over, his shoulder blades seemed to be pointing at them from across the barbed-wire fence.

Ruth didn't even look up from her cup where she was bobbing her teabag. The doctor had told her to stop eating so much chocolate and drinking so much coffee due to her ulcer. "That's Junior."

"He's getting too skinny," Dolores said and looked over her glasses at Ruth, meaning she, Ruth, was getting too skinny, too. "Here, eat one of these." She pushed a plate toward her friend and continued to stare at Junior. "He's no future farmer," she said and took another bite as he continued to hoe and Ruth continued to bob.

Ruth pointed to a centerpiece display on her cluttered kitchen table. It was colored Indian corn, four pieces tied together with a string so that if she wanted she could hang it on her front door. "He made me that."

Dolores held it up. Each cob was hardly larger than the size of the corn in Chinese food. She said something in Navajo about him not planting the seeds deep enough and then put it back on the table amid newspaper clippings, crossword puzzles, a horoscope book, a doll's dress Ruth had begun mending two years ago, and a racing form.

Ruth opened a pack of Sweet and Low, stirred it into her tea, and said something that wasn't discernable above the rattle of the swamp cooler.

Dolores began to mix some instant coffee. "What?"

Ruth slid a newspaper toward Dolores and pointed at the headline with one long, brown, arthritic finger. She then held her hands tightly together in front of her as if she were a child saying a desperate prayer. Clutching her hands was the only way she could keep her long fingers from moving like the legs of a spider and her arms from flying open as if she were conducting an orchestra.

Dolores picked up the paper that was dated several weeks past and read, "Prosthetic Leg Found in Corrales Ditch." This was not news to Dolores. Ruth had come by her house early last week. In fact, she had driven all the way into town just to tell her about the leg that had been found in the ditch near her home. But, more importantly, to tell her that she thought she knew who it belonged to.

"Who?" Dolores had asked.

"You know. He was in the hospital. The one that was in the rodeo."

Dolores closed her eyes and saw him, a good-looking, tall, young man who rode bulls. He'd been thrown, not from his bull, but from the back of a Ford pickup truck. The X-ray of his femur looked like bone that had been broken into new galaxies. He had cried like a child when they dressed his wound following the amputation. "I can't ride bulls anymore," he'd told the two nurses that saw their sons, both born and unborn, in him. "I can't dance."

Dolores looked up from the paper and back out at Junior. He was working on the next row. She briefly wondered if Ruth had forgotten that she already had shown her this, but she knew better as Ruth's fingers began to tap the table, the vein on the back of her hand moving side to side like a snake. She took another bite of sweet roll, chewed slowly, sipped loudly, and, trying to sound uninterested, said, "Did they find the rest of him?"

Ruth slid another paper toward Dolores and tapped a column on the left-hand side of page B-6 next to an advertisement for Discount Tire. The prosthetic leg had indeed been identified and indeed did belong to a Navajo male who lived in the Albuquerque area. However, local law officials were unable to locate the owner.

That's when Ruth had got up, and, without asking, Dolores followed her through the laundry room with its sweet smell of dryer sheets and Tide to the garage, where they stood now, looking at the Hefty trash bag. "It's his other leg."

"How did it get in here?"

"I caught it in the ditch last night—with a Zwiggler."

The Zwiggler was a fishing fly named for a friend Ruth had met at the casino, Albert Zwiggler. After losing most of their money, she and Albert would sit in the coffee shop at the casino and talk about fishing. He showed her how to make a lure that could catch anything. It had the iridescent colors of a fly's eyes, aqua blues and greens. "Nothing can resist it," he'd told her as he held it up in the light of the coffee shop at two o'clock in the morning.

"When did you catch it?"

"Last night," Ruth said. She'd made the fly with feathers and copper wire. And even though she'd heard coyotes barking on the mesa, she went out into the cool summer night with her dog and cat following behind her.

"Where did you catch it?"

"You know the place." Where the ditch gurgles around that slight bend. Where the brown water feeds the roots of the oldest cottonwood tree. "It gave quite a fight." It had nearly dragged her and her dog, who held to the back of her pants, into the ditch.

"Does it have a shoe on?"

"A boot. A Tony Lama. Size 13."

Dolores saw the young man the day he was leaving the hospital. He had lost weight and his once-tight Wranglers were baggy. He pulled on one cowboy boot. It was still dusty from being a rodeo star and a projectile. The other boot was in the corner holding up his prosthetic leg.

"What about the rest of him?" Even though neither one of them said anything more, they both knew that Ruth had barely been able to retrieve his leg from this world that wanted to devour everything. "What are you planning on doing with it? Are you expecting some type of reward?"

A smile briefly crossed Ruth's face, then it disappeared like a hawk diving behind that same cottonwood tree where she'd caught the leg. "I'm taking it to the family. If this was your son, wouldn't you want his leg?"

"You know where they live?"

Ruth took a piece of paper out of the front pocket of her loose jeans and handed it to Dolores.

It was in an older neighborhood in Albuquerque. Houses constructed of cinder block in the 1960s, near where Ruth and her family had lived before they had moved next to the blind Martinez's. The place she had wanted to leave to try and keep them safe from this sort of thing.

"Will you just leave it? What if a dog carries it off?"

"I've already called them. They're expecting us."

"Us?" Dolores said, along with something else in Navajo followed by a headshake and a "tsk."

Ruth hit the button for the trunk of her Ford Taurus, and it flew open like the lid of a casket. Together they put the bag inside and drove across the river toward town.

The house was on a street named after the home of another lost son and one of Ruth and Dolores's favorite recording artists, Graceland. They pulled up and both got out. The mother and father must have heard the car doors slam, because as Ruth and Dolores approached the house, they could see a big bear of a man standing behind the thin screen door. He towered over the two older women, who were dressed identically in navy-blue windbreakers with the IHS/PHS logo, elastic waist jeans, and New Balance athletic shoes. Without speaking the two women led him to the car and what was left of his son.

His son, who had taken first place in every roping competition he'd been in since the age of seven and had been the champion bull rider for four years straight at the Navajo Nation Fair. He'd worn a huge belt buckle stating he was a champ over his thin hips and was about to start a career in the PBR rodeo circuit.

Ruth pushed the button of the trunk as the mother, still behind the veil of the screen door, began to wail like only a mother who has lost a child can. The leg, which was triple bagged, still had the odor of a wound. Ruth took the Zwiggler lure off her fishing cap and placed it on the bag. The Zwiggler she'd made from the feathered earrings her daughter had left behind when she moved out, earrings made of peacock feathers, which are supposed to be good luck.

The man picked up the trash bag as if he were lifting a newborn out of a crib. He carried the leg like that same delicate newborn toward the cinder-block house painted the color of sand in the wash in Canyon de Chelly. The mother opened the door and let her husband and what was left of her beautiful son into the house.

Dolores and Ruth returned to the Ford Taurus, closing the heavy doors. Ruth sat behind the big steering wheel, and Dolores held to the door handle as they both looked toward the mesa where the volcanoes called the Seven Sleeping Sisters lay under a darkening sky.

The Sleeping Sisters, who that night dreamed of a boy who became a man, a bull rider and a fancy dancer who won all the pow wows and the heart of a woman who became his wife. Together they had a hundred children, formed a dancing troupe, and traveled the country, the world, the universe, dancing and laughing and dancing and laughing.

RED DIRT GIRL

Some critics say you should never start or even use a dream in a story, but I'm awake now and pretending that it wasn't a dream at all. We're out in the woods, as you call it, even though the trailer park is just beyond our view. You're reading from a romance novel you've stolen from the lady's house where you babysit. Found it where us girls always know to look for the things our mother's hide—in the laundry basket. Nobody but a woman ever sees the bottom of that. We're sharing an apple and a bag of potato chips, and your voice, to use old and lovely clichés, is like sunlight or moonshine warming my red clay heart, and I wonder how high is the price of admission to stay here forever? I don't think I'll ever have enough.

You hold the book closer to your green eyes and read, "He put his hand on the small of her back and pulled her toward him. She could feel the heat that was coming from his body, and even though Victoria couldn't breathe, she'd never felt more alive. He bent and kissed the hollow between her neck and shoulder. His breath was ragged and hot, and she knew that her life was about to change forever."

You pause, put a chip in your mouth, and smile at me. "Looks like Victoria's in love." The book dangles from your hand just above the creek. The water splashes up, and the sunlight that's not held by the overhanging poplar tree is caught and creates tiny rainbow sparks that land on your legs, legs that have gotten stronger from being forced to run track by your father when he caught you smoking cigarettes. I can tell by how deep the tan line is on your thigh and how high the creek is running that it's almost summer.

And before you begin to read again, before the dawn breaks through my bedroom window and pushes you back to your side of the world and me to mine, I try to become a swashbuckling pirate, a cowboy or the Indian, your hero or mine. Saving me from never knowing how to love.

I'm not sure there was a place called the High Noon
Moon. I think we might have dreamed this place up.
One Foot says it might have been that old bar behind the
Mountain That Moves, and that's what happened. It just
moved. I think we were in a spell.

—Mister

Live at the House of the High Noon Moon

Some of my songs are like dreams, and when you go to sleep at night you don't know if you're gonna have a dream or what you're gonna dream about.

—*Buffy Sainte-Marie*

I will tell you something about stories. They aren't just entertainment. They are all we have to fight off illness and death. You don't have anything if you don't haves stories.

—*Leslie Marmon Silko*

SHINE

As the fate of pennies goes, you turned up the other day—half-buried next to a 7-Up bottle cap and a ruined pack of matches from the El Vado Motel—a vintage Lincoln scolding me. "I fell out in 1983, out of that pocket you never mended, just allowing your change to fall all over the place. Tsk."

I retrieved you, never thinking that maybe there's no luck left in a tarnished penny from 1977: the year Elvis died, Father left, and I learned to disappear. Not knowing that maybe what I'm looking for is falling on me now like new snow, elm-seed husks chewed with prayers by a tiny brown sparrow.

That maybe the luck is not in this Lincoln who looks more tired than my mother, profile sagging under the weight of what cannot be recovered, but in the magic of licking silver thread, sticking it in the eye of a needle, mending holes with a simple and holy song.

BEST YEARS OF MY LIFE

Her mom met her at the front door, smiling, holding the screen door open with her long, thin arm.

She tried to smile back then stepped past her mom and the men's work boots on the floor in the entryway, put there by her mom to deter would-be intruders with the thought that a man lived in the house. "This is just a temporary situation," she said. Not that her mom had asked. Theirs was a family that did not need or particularly want explanations.

She followed her mom down the off-white hallway, devoid of family photos, to her old bedroom. The unique smell of her mother's home: dust, animals, and soap enveloped and overwhelmed her. Her mom turned on the overhead light and the popcorn ceiling glittered. She remembered studying this ceiling, imagining a night sky, searching for a pattern to emerge, a new constellation and myth.

She set her suitcase down on the avocado-green carpet, so old and flat it looked like a putting green in need of water. The room was last used by her sister's two sons in the early '90s, between their mom's first and second marriages. It was still decorated in early-American kindergartener, complete with macaroni pictures, dinosaur posters, and a ruler taped to the wall to measure the boy's height. Her sister had remarried and moved to Florida when the boys were three foot-two and four foot-one. They were in college now.

Her mom had already made up one of the twin beds. Her Mrs. Beasley doll decorated it because Indians never got rid of anything, or at least not these Indians. For example, their idea of a complete set of dishes were ones that had been collected through the years: the platter, two coffee cups, several saucers from the wedding set of China, and three dinner plates still intact bought with S&H green stamps. These were combined with two plastic children's dinner plates—one from the movie *The Lion King* (Rafiki holding up a young Simba) and one from *Beauty and the Beast* (the Beast dancing with Belle under a starry sky)—and a nearly full set of colorful dinnerware designed with bananas, apples, and a slice of watermelon that Mom received as a "gift" from the casino.

Her mom turned on the night light and returned to standing at the bedroom doorway, still smiling at her daughter. "I'm going to put on some tea. Would you like a cup?"

"I think I'll go to bed. I'm tired." This was a lie. As she trekked across the country, she'd lived on coffee and microwavable taquitos, not exactly an elixir for already-frayed nerves. Frayed from the drama and then the trauma of moving out of her and her partner of five years' house. Well, obviously it was her partner's house, but neither had acted adultlike during the move. Not even the cat, who jumped in the back of her truck camper and refused to get out, which was odd. The cat didn't even like her, but she'd taken his ottoman. It was *her* ottoman, she'd stated emphatically to Laura. Despite the tears and pleas of Laura to the cat, he wouldn't get out of the truck. He'd made his choice, but just as soon as she arrived at her mom's and opened the camper door, he made his escape.

"Don't worry about Mósí," her mom said. "She'll be back."

He. She thought about clarifying the cat's gender. And his name was Shadow, but her mom called all cats Mósí, and anyway, what was the point? Mósí would or wouldn't be back. Mósí, a city cat, would or wouldn't be eaten by a coyote tonight.

Her mom just kept smiling. Then she said good-night and closed the door behind her.

She put her clothes in the dresser. The same dresser her mom had painted lime green before the family had made its way into the middle class and purchased the French provincial bedroom suite. One headboard of the suite remained, along with the nightstand between the mismatched twin beds. The nightstand light was a house—a bakery from a Bavarian Christmas Village. The windows glowed bright and welcoming beside the most modern item in the room, a digital clock radio that read 9:32 even though it was 11:45. She set her overnight bag on the console TV that didn't work, beside the newer one that did if the rabbit-ears antennae were fiddled with long enough. She sat on the saggy twin bed and looked at Mrs. Beasley. She wondered for the first time about Beasley's husband. How long had they been married? Had she ever had her heart broken, been cheated on, or was this straw-haired, bespeckled, polka-dot-clad lady the heartbreaker? She pulled the string, and Beasley said in her wise little-old-lady voice, "I used to be a little girl, just like you."

Really? Somehow, she could not imagine Mrs. Beasley growing up here. She'd just had the misfortune of being shipped to Albuquerque, New Mexico, in the early '70s and becoming trapped in a bedroom with mauve blinds special ordered from Sears alongside her only other doll, Barbie's lesbian cousin, Francie. She couldn't see Beasley crying herself to sleep in this room for 496 consecutive nights like she had when her dad left. With a pillow over her face, just in case someone was listening (God)—she wouldn't be heard, wouldn't give him the satisfaction. She'd made tally marks in pencil on the wall until it got past 150.

"That's a long time for a kid, 496 nights," she said to Beasley. And preteen years were even longer. She was twelve on night number one. And because the Lord our God is such a just God, she got her period on that first night her dad didn't come home. Afraid to tell her mom, who seemed to be going off the deep end, she decided to pilfer her sister's tampons that were hidden under the bathroom sink. In those dark moments of that first night in the laundry room, she'd sat on the edge of the toilet seat smoking one of her father's stolen Pall Malls like she was already past her prime and wondering what she could have done differently to make her dad stay.

She came up with a few ideas. When he came to pick her up, she'd make sure she was doing something like pulling weeds, or she'd wave a dishrag out the door and yell, "Just a minute—I'm finishing the dishes," or she'd make sure the living-room window was open so he could hear from outside the gate (he was no longer allowed in the yard) the vacuum cleaner running back and forth across the avocado-green carpet. A final touch would be to spray lemon-scented furniture polish on herself like perfume to give the subliminal message that he had just caught her in the middle of dusting. (She'd read the olfactory nerve was the only cranial nerve that went directly to the brain and caused emotional reactions.)

Alas, after 496 nights it was clear Dad wasn't coming back. She'd found the divorce papers while doing some investigative work, i.e., looking through her mom's drawers for clues as to how her father, the president of their church, and her mother, a mezzo-soprano in the church choir, could be getting a divorce.

But there it was, the proof, the divorce papers wadded up in her hand and being set on fire. Now she'd have to come clean to her friends, tell them Dad wasn't in Africa on mission work, he wasn't visiting sick relatives, his appendix was fine—he just wasn't coming home. He was gone, living on the other side of the river, and she began to remove him from her memory.

Her mom had asked at some point, "What happened to all the pictures of your father?" She had shrugged and didn't tell Mom that for their own good she had made a time capsule and buried it at 35.232754 longitude, 106.663044 latitude.

She wondered if—? She stood up and opened the bifold closet doors. Sure enough, on the top shelf was a dusty envelope. She remembered this stationary; she'd thought it so pretty, yellow sheets with bees flying around the edges, flowers in the corners. She recognized too the penciled *X* that marked the burial site. She looked at Beasley then quietly opened and crawled out the window that had no screen. It was chilly, late September, and her breath hung in the air. The weeds that had grown up in the old garden were dry and crunched under her steps. A creature scurried away from her.

"Shadow," she whispered, practically hissed. "Shadow." Nothing else moved, so she proceeded.

The garden gate, amazingly still latched, not so amazingly leaned to one side once unlatched. She scraped her hand against the stucco house lifting it up and opening it, sucking on her bloody knuckle, and then she crept into the backyard past the sliding-glass door. Light from the TV flickered in the den. At the side of the garage was the same old shovel, the wooden handle as smooth as a walking stick.

She had thought about burying the time capsule somewhere in the middle of the mesa, but, like her mom, she had a hard time getting rid of stuff. She paced off steps that matched her twelve-year-old feet. Once she knew she was in the right place (because the rock she'd set over it, of course, was still there), she dug. It was mainly sand on that side, so it didn't take her very long. About two feet down she hit the metal box and pulled it out. Using her phone's flashlight, she sat on the low wall surrounding the old well and opened it. Inside was her parent's wedding photo. Her mom was thin, no stoop to the shoulders. Beautiful. Her father, handsome in his simple black suit and navy haircut. The photo was black and white, but she could see his blue eyes. Also in the box was the first-place ribbon she'd won at the State Fair for her Taco Supreme, her dad's favorite recipe that she had made for him on certain Sundays. A turquoise and coral bracelet he'd given her on her tenth birthday. The newspaper clipping from when she'd come in first in the city-wide free-throw contest in her age category. He stood next to her with his arm over her shoulder. She held the ball that was the prize under her arm. That was the last thing she'd ever won.

She lit the joint that was also in the time capsule, took a deep drag, and coughed. She blew the smoke toward the brightest star.

Her dad had left in the summer. Getting her period, and him leaving, signaled childhood was over, but she didn't know what to do with her interminable adult daylight hours. She read, practiced free throws, watched *Phil Donahue* and *The Merv Griffin Show*, went for walks with her mom when she got home from work, picked up aluminum cans along the ditch, pushed her bike to the paved road and rode across the river. Something her dad had told her never to do. Traffic whizzed by, and her handlebars stuck out so far in the road that she could feel the brush of death on her knuckles.

One day, it must have been the middle of summer because the day had gone on forever, she rode her bike across the river and then south to Central Avenue. Central opened wide toward the mountain, and from there she could see the only skyscraper in Albuquerque, the eighteen-story First National Bank. The bank was five miles to the east of the river, and her father's new house was another three miles up from the bank, in "the heights," where people moved to have a view. She started up the avenue, part of the old Route 66, riding on the gum-pocked sidewalk, stopping for lights and maneuvering around the homeless people and the Moonies. From the valley to the foothills the change in elevation was fifteen hundred feet. She'd thought she'd been training her whole life for the Olympics, to be a gold-medal basketball player, but no, this was what she'd been training for, to ride to her father's new home.

Her legs churned and burned until finally she got to the street that lead to his house. On the corner was the newest high school in the city; "Home of the Conquistadors" was painted on the side wall of the school, along with a man on a horse, both in shiny metal armor. He'd unsheathed his sword and held it out, pointing at her. She spit on the road and kept riding, through the landscaped neighborhood with flowers in terra-cotta pots thriving in the shaded entrances of the homes. Dogs barked but were effectively contained behind backyard gates. The grass in front yards grew thick, minimizing blowing sand, so that when windows were opened, they didn't stick at all.

She slid one open easily and entered her dad's house. She stood in his bedroom. Well, his and his new wife's bedroom. It smelled like him though. She sunk into the orange shag carpet. She walked around in her father's house as if it were her own. She got a glass of orange juice, sat and read the newspaper at the large dining-room table. Looked through the cabinets and didn't see any of his favorite foods like Ritz crackers and sardines, only saltines. She chewed one as she carefully examined his new life hanging in the hallway. She stared at his smiling face. "Liar," she said, and she wasn't sure if it was this picture she was referring to or the one that she brought with her and thumbtacked to the wall with the rest of the "family" photos. It was the original of her and him after she won the free-throw contest.

Then she crawled back out the window and rode home.

She wondered how long it would take her dad, and Barbra, to find the photo. She imagined the trouble she'd be in. Was breaking and entering a crime if your father lived there? She wondered how many years in the clink she'd get for trespassing. But she never heard anything about the "unwarranted infringement." Nothing except that same evening her mom said her father had called and asked about her. Wondered if she were all right.

"Just fine, Dad." Her words, visible in the cold September night, hung in front of her like smoke. It'd been over thirty years since she'd buried the time capsule, five years after her family moved from the city, out of a little cinder-block house to their custom-built three-bedroom "rancher" on nearly an acre in what used to be the "country." She looked up at the stars. It all seemed so permanent, so fixed. She couldn't remember when she'd learned that stars are born through gravitational instability, through collision and collapse. Born under the cloak of night, millions of years away, until finally their wobbly light reaches Earth.

She reburied the box. Like the north star, she'd always know where to find it. She put the shovel against the garage, walked around back. The TV still flickered, her mom still up in her chair watching back-to-back reruns of *MASH*, waiting in that house, waiting for her children to come home.

Shadow was sitting on the windowsill cleaning a paw when she returned. "Mósí."

He looked at her, unfazed, like all he really cared about was his ottoman. She went back to retrieve it from the camper, maneuvered it through the window while he watched from the unmade twin. She crawled back in and placed the ottoman beneath her oldest nephew's kindergarten-graduation picture. "There," she said to him. "Your home." He jumped on top and batted at the faded blue-and-white tassel with the charm, "'95."

She laid down on the bed opposite him and stared at the ceiling. It glittered by the light of the Bavarian bakery. She switched off the light.

She picked up Beasley and looked at her. "Just one night," she told her. Then she put the pillow over her face and cried.

SYMPATHY FOR THE DEVIL

We were sitting at the Fat Chance on Central Avenue across the street from the University of New Mexico. Eerbie and I would go there on Thursday nights to listen to the woman who sang tobacco-and-whiskey-infused songs. Pitchers of beer were three dollars, and I think I was in love with her and the place. She was not beautiful, not like Eerbie, but they both had voices that had learned to hold attention in dark and smoky places.

While she was singing, Eerbie was talking, Eerbie was always talking—he's like the wind here in Albuquerque—it may be just a breeze, but it rarely stops blowing.

That evening he shouted over the noise of the bar and our singer. "You know little Cuz, we were both born on a day when the sky was all shot up."

I looked at him and shook my head, "Eerbie, you were born on a beautiful day in August." I returned to listening to our singer and her rendition of the Stones tune she was covering. God, I wish I could remember her name. She was balanced on the edge of a high barstool, one booted foot set firmly on the stage and the other hooked on the bottom rail. She cradled a twelve-string Ovation guitar to her breasts.

Eerbie yelled, "No, our day got tattooed with a pink pillbox hat, black Cadillacs, and blood."

Eerbie always told this story when he got dumped, pointing to the fictitious day of his birth as the reason for his being unable to keep a lover.

I looked at him. His long brown fingers were gently wrapped around the lukewarm glass of beer, and he took a sip as if it were fine Chablis. I wish I'd known then that he would be gone in just two short years. I would have paid more attention, but then again, I can say that about a lot of things.

Eerbie continued, "My dad was there, waiting for me to be born at the Presbyterian's hospital. He was dressed in his best western wear, a green short-sleeve shirt, brown Lee western pants that hung at the perfect length over the tops of his alligator and kangaroo cowboy boots. All the nurses were checking him out as he stood in the corner of the waiting room smoking a Pall Mall."

Eerbie lit a cigarette and took a long drag.

"In the waiting room with Dad there was a grandma. She was sitting across from him knitting a baby blanket, the needles clicking together like a metronome. She had on a traditional velveteen blouse, a pleated skirt, and a squash-blossom necklace that weighed about ten pounds." He paused to take a drag and for me to turn and look at him. His eyes were squinting through the smoke as it rose and twirled over our heads.

"Then the news came over the speakers that the president was shot.

"My dad just stood there, opening and closing his silver Zippo lighter. My mom, who was being wheeled down the cold cinder-block hallway to the delivery room, picked up her little head and questioned if she'd heard that right, but when the orderly who was pushing the gurney fainted, she knew she had.

"And the grandma stopped knitting and began to rock back and forth in her chair."

I strained to hear our singer—Sally, that was her name. I yelled to Eerbie, "This is her last song before break, just let me—"

But he continued, "My mom cried, tears rolled down her cheeks and into her ears. She cried not just because she was in god-awful pain or because she loved that president, but because even though she always said she wasn't a very good Indian, she knew this was a bad sign, to have a child born on such a day. Oh, the bad luck the child would carry. Ee-yah. Meanwhile the grandma in the waiting room with Dad began to cry, too."

The people in the bar got up and started dancing, obscuring Sally from my view, so I turned all the way around in my booth and scowled at Eerbie.

"Did she cry loudly," I asked him even though I knew this story by heart. It was, after all, my birth story, embellished through the years by Eerbie and his broken hearts.

"Oh little Cuz, that shooting opened a flood gate in her, and you know that doesn't happen too often to us Indians."

Which wasn't true. Eerbie cried at the drop of a hat.

I took a sip of beer and asked him, "What did your dad do?"

"He stood there speechless, as still as a cowboy watching his last sunset, wishing he could have a beer, but he lit another cigarette instead and looked out the dusty window into the parking lot."

Then Eerbie pretended to be speechless, and we both gazed into our nearly empty beer glasses as if they were crystal balls. Inside was a grassy knoll and a dead lawn, hazy footage of a presidential parade and a family vacation, a child saluting a casket being pulled by horses, and horses fast approaching with riders that carried guns and blankets warmed with fever. We heard children laughing as they played kick-the-can and a lonely person crying.

Sally was coming to the end of her song and strumming hard, breaking six of her twelve strings; the dancers were dancing like it was the last round at the All Indian Pow-Wow.

I finished my beer and asked, as if I didn't know, "And then what happened?"

Eerbie took a long drag of his cigarette and blew smoke up and over my head, and we smiled at one another. He had a piece of tobacco stuck between his two front teeth. "The grandma stopped rocking in her chair, and her knitting fell to the floor. Then she looked up through the ceiling, through the orthopedic and geriatric wards, through blue sky and on into the heavens—"

Eerbie and I looked up with her. Through the dingy ceiling of the Fat Chance Bar and Grill, through the stars we could see and the wormholes we couldn't, and we all cried, "Why couldn't it have been Eisenhower?"

FLYING HIGH AGAIN

Every summer our tribe held a race to see which clan could fly the fastest and farthest. Under section C, article twelve of the Fourth Sacred Law, it clearly stated that "The People can fly, but only on shields and *only* when the moon is full." The exception was the Sparrow Clan, who were to be the referees of the race.

The Bat Clan had won the race for the past three hundred years. This made the Antelope Clan very angry, for they were known for quick action and athletic ability. They couldn't see how the Bats—old women who sat around in the dark telling stories and smoking pipes—could beat them year after year. The more they thought about it, the more it became clear that the Bats were cheating. So they would cheat too. The Antelopes got together with Coyote and made a plan.

It was high noon in the middle of the hottest day of the year. The Sparrows sat in a piñon tree eating nuts at the base of the Fourth Sacred Mountain. The Antelopes came out of their hogan with their flying shields. They sat down on the dirt road and waited for the moon to come up. The Bats were in their hogan, sipping coffee, smoking pipes, and talking about all the races they'd won over the years. The Bats weren't worried, because they were good friends with Sister Moon. They'd give her some tobacco, and she'd tell them just exactly when she'd be arriving.

So when the moon came up and sat on top of the mountain in the middle of the day, it was a big surprise. The chief of the Sparrow Clan spat out a nut and yelled, "Let the race begin."

The Antelopes took off on their shields, rising swiftly until they were only specks in the blue summer sky. The Sparrows flew into the Bats' hogan. It was so filled with smoke and so dark they could barely see. They told the Bats, "The moon is out. The Antelopes are winning the race."

The Bats, not expecting to fly for another four nights, readied themselves by making another pot of coffee.

Meanwhile, the rest of the tribe, comprised of the Spider Clan and the Lizard Clan, who had forgotten how to fly a long time ago, gathered around to look up into the sky. They marveled at how quickly the young Antelopes were traveling. They began to gossip about the Bats, saying that they were too old and had begun to make mistakes.

The sun was setting when the Bats finally came out. They looked to the top of the Fourth Sacred Mountain and said, "If that's the moon, why is the sun setting right next to it?"

The People went silent. The Bats were right. That wasn't the moon. The Antelopes and Coyote had tricked them. They'd stolen the sacred shield from Grandfather's hogan. Crafty Coyote used a piece of mica to reflect the sun so that the old, nearly transparent hide of the shield looked like a summer moon atop the mountain. They thought they were pretty clever until the sacred shield and Coyote's tail caught fire. Coyote howled and howled.

In fact, he's still howling at the Antelopes about his burnt tail.

The young Antelopes never made it any farther. They were frozen into stars in the northern sky—frozen in the shape of a bat. A reminder of what can happen if the sacred laws are broken. A reminder to always, always listen like an old Bat.

The Econoline gave up the ghost for good in 1983. Luckily, we were on our "acoustic tour" and were only traveling with the bare bones of the band. We unloaded our gear and walked back to the interstate. You can still see her rusted shell at the base of Blue Bead Mountain. She became part of that mountain again.

—*One Foot*

S

Live at the House of Yellow Butterfly Girl

There is no "us" and "them"; it's an illusion.
—*Roger Waters*

I'll tell you a secret. Old storytellers never die. They disappear into their own story.
—*Vera Nazarian*

MAY THIS BE LOVE

Red Clay Man emerged from the bank of the dry wash with sprigs of tamarisk in his hair and dirt beneath his fingernails. PFC Lewis Nelwood, or Red Clay Man, as his buddies in the marines called him, had been a fine-looking man. He could have taken any pow wow contest just by flashing his once-pearly whites. But now he's wrecked, like an old truck that got sideswiped. And him only twenty-five.

This morning, as he walked toward the rising sun, he heard a water song. Sung by a turquoise stone, set in the bracelet he carried in the front pocket of his flak jacket beneath his Purple and broken heart. And even though the bracelet was wrapped in an old sock, he could still hear the music. It rarely stopped.

The bracelet was his grandfather's. He had not been a religious man, not traditional, except for a few things like wearing your jewelry to meet your creator. His family had planned to bury the bracelet, but Lewis told himself that someone would just dig up the grave the way they do and steal it. And then one day Lewis might be walking around like a normal human being, at the grocery store or at the Navajo Nation Fair, and he'd see it—the stone—winking at him from some other man's wrist, and he might kill him, or at least beat the shit out of him. Because there are some things that can't be controlled for long. Things like anger, thieves, and water. Maybe for a while they can be staved off with meditation or medication, with burglar alarms and shotguns, with dams and mills, but sooner or later anger erupts and kills or maims, thieves rob graves or boldly take something precious and personal off a limp wrist, and water floods the valley or drowns you with songs that are so sweet and haunting, a wounded soul can't survive it.

Sometimes the stone would sing a blues version of "I Wish It Would Rain," and it reminded him of the light rain that hung over the desert the morning his mother passed away. Other times it would sing a song that was nearly forgotten except by the very old, like his grandfather—104 when he died. The song carried with it the smell of the river up north where they used to fish when he was a little boy.

Sometimes Lewis would take out the bracelet when this song was being sung and close his eyes. He could see his grandfather standing nearly waist deep in water, fishing pole held high, a wicker basket tied to his narrow hips and filled with fish even though the sun was barely above the canyon wall. He saw himself, Lewis, standing on the bank with a cup collecting minnows and water spiders. Behind him smoke from the campfire and steam from the coffee pot twirled up, not gray but silver, into a sky that momentarily reminded him of innocence.

Lewis looked up now into a similar sky. Two turkey vultures rode updrafts, circling higher and higher in the cool air. So cool, the vultures might travel twenty thousand feet, nearer to heaven than Lewis would ever be.

He pulled the sock out of his pocket, took out the bracelet, and offered it to the vultures. He yelled at them, "Tell him I'm sorry. I'm so sorry." But the vultures were already black specks, and the sky swallowed his cries whole.

He felt sweat under his arms even though he was shivering. A loud clap of thunder roared through his mind as the last in the triune rotation of songs sung to him by the stone began, as soft and sweet as a lullaby at first, then followed by a strange high-pitched instrument that whined, and he was no longer in the desert, or on the banks of the river up north skipping stones. He was standing in mud, in the jungle of Vietnam, and it was raining—always raining—and people that looked like him, his aunties and cousins, his family, except smaller with delicate bones like birds, stared at him. And he can't tell if they're crying or if it's just the rain as smoke rises from grass huts that not even a torrent can extinguish.

He fell to his knees, picked up sand, and rubbed it between his hands, repeating to himself, "You're home. You're home now." He repeated it over and over and told himself they didn't have rabbit brush in Vietnam. "Look—that's Blue Bead Mountain." Pristine, with ponderosa pines at the top with trunks bigger round then Uncle Eddy. "You can see for miles."

Not in the jungle. These are your people. But how many nights did he wake to find his wife beating his back and arms while he pulled the covers off their bed, turning over the mattress, yelling at her, "Where are they? Where are the guns?" And a baby—his baby—cries in the chaos of screams.

"I'm sorry. I'm so sorry," he'd tell his wife later, but she pulled away, frightened of him—he was frightened of him—and no matter how much wood he chopped or vodka he drank, no matter if he passed out cold, it was never enough. So he started sleeping outside, farther and farther away from her and their son, afraid he might hurt them, afraid that he'd become part of a storm, afraid that he was not the wind or the rain, not the thunder or the rainbow, but the place that is struck by lightning.

Harold Montgomery drove into town on that crystal-clear Sunday morning after one of the worst thunderstorms to hit Gallup in ten years. It seemed like the earth had shaken most of the night. His two-year-old daughter and the family dog were so scared they had to sleep in bed with him and his wife, Clare. So this morning he was surprised that he could make it down the road between his ranch and into town at all. Oftentimes with that much rain no one could get a vehicle, even a plow, in and out for days. Just had to wait for the mud to dry and the thin layer of clay that covered the ground to curl up into a thousand of what looked like cruel smiles. "Early Morning Rain" played on the radio in his brand-new two-tone Ford F-250, and he was in a fine mood. He'd gotten himself out of going to church, and the potluck that followed, by telling his wife he'd better check the alarm at the shop since the power had been out for a good six hours.

Harold lit a cigarette and rolled down the window. A cool breeze tousled his thin brown hair, and he thought how the sky looked as if it had been scrubbed clean—not that it was ever dirty here in this high desert. He blew smoke out the window, took a swig of Jack Daniel's from the flask he kept in the glove box, and thought of Jeannie with the light-brown hair, or black hair, or blonde hair depending on which wig she chose to wear on any given night or day. He smiled to himself. On several occasions he'd told her, "I wish you'd just wear your hair natural, Jean," and once he'd tugged playfully at the top of the wig. She'd quickly swatted his arm away and told him that wigs were very much in style, very sophisticated.

He knew there was another reason. Maybe she was bald. But Harold didn't care. Jean was all he ever thought about, what he was thinking about as he neared the turn off the highway and noticed a green lump laying off the road a good fifty feet. He thought that it was awful far back from the road for a duffel bag to land if it had fallen off the back of a truck.

"Just keep going," the little voice in his head, the one that he rarely listened to, said.

He stopped the truck and slowly backed up.

He got out and walked through the sagebrush, sinking into the mud. Sweat began to bead on his forehead. His belly, which hung too far over his belt, turned over a time or two. He took out the handkerchief he kept in his back pocket and wiped his neck.

Harold stood over not a bag, but a body. With no shoes on. Lying face down.

"Shit."

He generally carried a revolver tucked between his pants belt and his back, but he'd left it in the glove box. He looked around. There wasn't a thing for miles, not a cow or a sheep in sight, and it was dead quiet. The calm after the storm, he thought.

He nudged the body with the tip of his boot. It didn't budge. His images of Jean dissipated into the blue sky up above the two vultures that were circling.

He bent down, turned the body over, and jumped back. "Shit."

The skin on the man's face and chest were marked with what looked like purple or black lace. He had a hole, much like a bullet wound, on his chest, near his heart, and then the same thing on the bottom of one foot. His eyes, or where they once were, were orbs of darkness.

"Struck by lightning, poor bastard," Harold said. He felt a tightness in his chest. There was no way Harold would be able to get the body in the back of the truck by himself even if he tried, which he wasn't going to do. He wiped his neck again. He pulled a cigarette out of his front pocket, lit it, and exhaled deeply. He looked around again as he had the distinct feeling he was being watched.

He bent down on one knee and checked the guy's pants pocket for ID. The wallet was worn thin. Six dollars, a photo of a baby, and probably a much younger version of the man with his skinny arm draped over a women's shoulders. He grinned at Harold.

Harold put the wallet back in his pocket, looked around. Behind a sagebrush was a boot; another lay about forty feet farther off.

"Shit, that had to have stung."

He laid the boots by the dead man's feet and was on his way back to his truck when he spotted a green sock and went to retrieve it. It contained something. Something heavy.

Harold shook the bracelet out of the sock. Under the clear morning sun it seemed to wink at him.

Harold had had a heart attack several years ago. As he took a drag off his cigarette and looked more closely at the bracelet, he felt a slight pang in his chest. He stuck the cigarette between his lips and pulled out the little bottle of nitroglycerin tablets he kept in the same pocket as his cigarettes, unscrewed the tiny cap with his large fingers, shook two out into his palm, and put them under his tongue to dissolve. He looked again at the bracelet through smoke that curled up from the Pall Mall.

The piece was very old, heavy sand-casted silver, and the turquoise looked to be from the old Cerrillos mine. It was worth a pretty penny, and it created a dilemma for Harold. At least, he tried to make it one.

Leave it here with the body and wait for the county coroner, who often brought pieces into Harold's pawnshop, to bring it in—or not. It was certainly a piece that a person would want to keep. He looked at the body and wondered why the guy was carrying it in a sock. He was probably headed to the pawnshop with it anyway.

Put it back.

Harold crushed out his cigarette and rolled the body back over to buy the guy a little time from the two vultures that were circling closer to the ground, then he twisted the bracelet onto his thick wrist. His flesh pushed out between the fine entrails of the sand-casted silver, and the turquoise winked at him again. He turned the engine and the air conditioning on high and leaned his head back against the back window of the cab, waiting for the nitroglycerin to dissolve as Hank Williams sang about someone crying in the rain.

Jean pulled at the hem of her miniskirt. She'd made it herself, and it was a little tighter than she'd meant for it to be and may have been a little over the top for a summer night in Gallup, but what the hell. As the wind blew her in the door to the motel, she waved back to Harold who was already driving his El Dorado around to the back.

She rang the bell on the counter and was met by a young woman, a girl, really, whom she'd never seen before. Jean looked at her red plastic name tag. Muriel. Muriel wore her thin blonde hair pulled back in a ponytail and had several attractive freckles on her small nose. She wore a pair of black-framed glasses that she quickly took off and placed on the counter near the phone book. She had light-blue eyes with shallow crow's feet in the corners from squinting, as she did at Jean now.

Jean cleared her throat and said, "Room 123, if it's available. Please." She held her head high, as if she were checking into the Ritz Carlton instead of the Ranchito Motel. Her voice was deep and controlled, practiced many times in front of mirrors, the first of which was when she was just child, a little boy looking into the compact stolen out of her auntie's purse.

Muriel squinted at her.

Jean looked over the woman's head at the pegboard. The key to room 123 dangled in its usual place.

"Do I know you?" Muriel asked.

Jean didn't answer but thought about the possibility. Jean's most recent job was at the Chat-N-Chew, where she was Chuck, not Jean. She wore the same uniform that all the men, or boys, who worked there wore: white button-up short-sleeved shirt and black polyester pants. Her long black hair was braided and worn under a white paper hat, not in a bouffant.

Jean cleared her throat and smiled, teeth so white they really could be in the mouth of a beauty queen. "Where's Wayne?" Wayne was the night-shift manager that had a crush on her and let her have the room for less.

"He got fired. He was letting his friends go back to Room 68 and watch color TV. For free."

"I see."

Muriel continued to squint at Jean. "You look so familiar to me."

"Well—Muriel—do you recall Miss Navajo Nation, 1969?"

Muriel shook her head.

Jean looked at the young woman over the top of her large sunglasses. She wore them despite the fact that it was already dark and the neon signs on Route 66 were blinking with a false sense of excitement. "My fry bread, along with my sheep-butchering technique, took the contest." They continued to look upon one another, Jean over her sunglasses and Muriel through her myopic eyes. "You don't believe me. I know what you're thinking. What is Miss Navajo 1968 doing in a dump like this?"

"'69."

"Yes, '69. Well. Sheep butchering only gets you so far, honey. I advise nursing school." Jean laid a ten-dollar bill on the counter. Rooms were 9.99 with tax. Wayne had let her have it for eight dollars. She wondered briefly if that had factored into his getting fired.

Muriel opened the night envelope, took a penny out, and placed it on the counter.

"The key."

"Sorry." Muriel got the key down from the peg and placed it next to the penny.

Jean unzipped her clutch purse, dropped the penny inside, and scooped the key up in her large hand. "Thank you," she said, holding her head high. With the bouffant wig and high heels, she was nearly six feet tall. "Have a good evening," and she turned to walk off—always a trick in heels.

Muriel called behind her, "Ma'am—are you—?"

Jean stopped and looked back, "Yes?"

Muriel's eyes widened. Her pale complexion suddenly turned rosy, even under the glare of the halogen lights. "Are you a Ronnette?"

"A Ronnette?"

"You know," and Muriel began to snap her fingers and sing the first few lines of "Walking in the Rain."

Now it was Jean's turn to stare at the young woman. Muriel was looking up at the stained asbestos-tile ceiling as if there were rain clouds actually floating above her head. Jean moved back toward the desk, marveling at Muriel's voice. Forgetting herself, she began to snap her fingers. Before she knew it the two of them were standing together behind the desk, harmonizing. Their voices transported them far past the Formica countertop, the flashing "Vacancy" sign, and the red rocks to the east, along the actual highway of dreams that had nothing to do with that road outside the motel. If anyone had walked in, they would have seen two young woman singing—dreaming, really—of love.

They finished and smiled broadly at one another.

Muriel flushed even more deeply, the freckles on her nose darkening. She sighed. "My mama loved that song. She played it every day, even after the record warped."

Jean held her hand out to Muriel. "I'm Veronica."

"I knew it," Muriel said, and slapped the top of the counter. "I said to myself when I saw you get out of that Cadillac, in that dress, 'now *there's* someone famous.'"

Jean smiled broadly and placed one large brown hand over Muriel's soft white one. "We have to keep it our little secret. Okay?" Jean realized just then that, with this lie, she was going to have to start staying at the more expensive Travel Lodge on the other side of town. But it was worth it.

"Of course," Muriel said, and she made the gesture her granny used all the time, ticking a lock on the lips.

Jean opened her clutch. She put the penny she had received as change from her ten-dollar bill back on the counter. Then she thought twice about the tip a Ronnette would leave and added another fifty cents. "Keep the change, Honey."

And this time, as she turned to leave, it was a little easier to navigate the heels, the door, and the wind that blew her around the corner toward Room 123 and Harold.

It was a clear night, so Muriel locked the motel cashbox and went outside to the gravel parking lot of the motel with her transistor radio, antennae pointed west in the general vicinity of San Francisco, trying to dial in 106.9 KMPX. Her favorite DJ was on from eight to twelve. She'd taken her hair out of its tight ponytail, certain her boss wasn't going to come by and check on things. He trusted her.

The parking lot was nearly empty this Sunday night. Only two station wagons, a pickup, and of course the Ronnette's Cadillac. She wished she *had* someone to tell, that the lead singer of the Ronnette's was staying at the Ranchito of all places—probably on her way to California. Muriel herself had high hopes of getting out of this "no-horse town," as her granny called it, and moving to California. She was saving every dime she could from working the night shift at the front desk and cleaning rooms in the morning. Veronica's secret would be safe with Muriel, that was for sure. Anyway, who would she tell? Her granny, who was the only person at home, wouldn't know a Ronnette from a hole in the ground. If something wasn't on *The Lawrence Welk Show*, *As The World Turns*, or *The Lutheran Hour* it was of no use to Granny.

Muriel moved the dial back and forth on her radio. It squelched and crackled. Just as she had tuned in the station, and as "May This Be Love" came over the long-distance airwaves, she heard the gun shot.

It wasn't as loud as you might think on a night like this, so crystal clear that KMPX could be heard broadcasting from atop a mountain in California. But it did scare her. It scared her enough that she dropped her radio, busting the back of it so that the 9-volt battery hung off the back by a blue wire. But Jimi Hendrix kept playing, kept singing about how nothing could harm him. Muriel picked it up and ran back to the front desk.

She was sure the shot had come from Room 123. Her first thought was that a Ronnette had been killed at her motel. She picked up the phone with a surprisingly steady hand and dialed the number her manager had taped to the counter for the Gallup Police Department.

The phone rang and rang. So she redialed, but still no answer. By this time, since nobody had run out of any of the rooms, she thought that maybe she'd just imagined it, or it had been an old truck backfiring on the highway, or a—

But just then she saw him. A young man, wearing what looked to be a Chat-N-Chew uniform—white shirt, black pants, and white paper hat—running out of Room 123. He had blood coming from a split lip, and his eye was nearly sealed shut with a bruise. But even with a half of his face swollen, even without the wig and the beautiful sequined dress, she could tell it was Veronica. She ran out into the parking lot.

Veronica was nearly to the road when she saw Muriel. She stopped and looked back at her.

Muriel saw the tears running down that swollen face, and she, Muriel, who had spent her twenty-one years believing what her granny had told her, that it was better not to know the truth, in that moment knew everything, not only about a boy dressed like a fabulous woman, but about herself.

She held up her hand to him and waved him away, saying softly to herself, "Go while you still can."

Veronica turned, adjusted her paper hat, and with head down walked out to the highway as Muriel ran into Room 123.

It's true that at one point Muriel had had aspirations of becoming a medical doctor like Dr. Susan Stewart on *As The World Turns*. But even Dr. Stewart had to deal with an alcoholic, cheating husband, so she figured, why bother going to college? She could head down to the Wagon Wheel on any given night and find that.

Muriel stood for a moment at the door and knocked. The door creaked open. It looked like every other one at the Ranchito, except for the dead man lying on the floor with his pants around his ankles.

Muriel had seen a dead body before, when she was ten. Her mama was still around and had taken her to the hospital to visit her granny, who'd had her gallstones removed. Her roommate, who was just as old as her granny, had been sitting up eating her dinner when suddenly she gasped as if excited about something, threw her head back violently, and immediately turned blue. But not as blue as this man, whose face was actually purple. But there was no blood on his body. Just a gun lying beside his head and a bullet hole through the bathroom door. There was blood on the bed. Once it dried it would blend right into the rusty-red color in the pattern of the bedspread. Also on the bed were Veronica's beautiful dress, her brunette wig, and a turquoise bracelet.

To this day Muriel's still not sure what made her do it. She picked up the bracelet and put it on. The "Vacancy" light over the office blinked through a crack in the drapes and made it seem as if the stone were a blue-green eye that glistened with a tear. She realized she was still carrying her radio, and even though it wasn't on she could hear a song about a rainbow—a rainbow calling her.

Muriel bent down and picked the gun up from beside the man's head. She took out his wallet. "Harold Montgomery" was what the driver's license read. She put the identification back but took the large roll of bills in his front pocket. She pulled her hair back in a ponytail, picked up the wig, and pulled it snugly on her head. It smelled of woman's perfume and sweat. She tucked the dress under her arm, put the gun in her waistband, and took his keys off the dresser.

She opened the door of Room 123 cautiously and looked up and down the cement walk in front of the rooms. Nobody. She closed the door quietly and walked to the Cadillac with her head held high and a swing to her hips. Before she got in the car she looked up at the sky. Even though the motel was right off the highway and the neon lights of Route 66 were as bright as a mini galaxy, there still seemed to be a million or more stars over her head. As she got in the car and quietly shut the heavy door, she thought of her granny. She'd lived with her since her mama had run off with the Charlie Chip man when she was sixteen. And her daddy? Well, he'd never even seen fit to pull his eighteen-wheeler over and stay the night after he got her mama pregnant with Muriel.

She sank into the plush seat that was softer than her mattress at home. She put the key in the ignition, turned it, and listened to the engine start up on the first try, unlike Granny's Buick that had to have the carburetor primed every time she started it. Muriel put the shifter in reverse, turned the big car toward the highway, and slowly pulled out, gravel crunching under the tires.

She went slowly, then she pressed the gas pedal harder as she reached the edge of town and the lights began to disappear behind her. She hoped forever. With any luck she could be in San Francisco in time tomorrow to watch the sunset over the bay.

She thought again of her Granny, probably just turning off the radio after listening to the rebroadcast of *The Lutheran Hour*. She thought of the long hours Muriel had sat outside the screen door of their little house on top of the hill—waiting. Waiting for her mama or daddy to come home and tell her they missed their baby. Most evenings Granny would come outside and sit with her and wait until the crickets came on, playing a tune of their very own, and the first evening star began to twinkle.

Granny had pointed at the star. "See that, Muriel? You can count on it to show up, but that's about all. I don't know if it's different in other places, but out here in the desert you're best not to get too attached to any one thing. A good rain could wash it all away."

With the push of a button, Muriel opened the driver-side window of the big Cadillac and stuck her elbow out. Cold air rushed in and slapped her in the face, and she laughed at it as the perfume on the wig wrapped itself around her. The bracelet felt good and heavy on her wrist, and she pushed the accelerator a little farther down as she looked up at the sky with its millions of stars.

Even though there wasn't a cloud in the sky, she thought it smelled like rain.

(SITTIN' ON) THE DOCK OF THE BAY

The first time I saw one of my parents cry is embedded like a silicon chip in my amygdala. It glints and sparks even as other memories that surround it erode. I'm sure when I die, when I'm burned to a crisp in the incinerator at French's Mortuary, the chip will remain.

I hope when my time comes, I'm not left in some cardboard container sealed shut with yellow crime tape like I saw at a patient's house one afternoon. The brown cylinder with Grandma in it sat among an array of dusty tequila bottles that seemed to be more cherished than her.

"No. You're telling me that's your mother in there?"

"She wanted a huge funeral," her daughter said as the mechanical lift of her chair whined, bringing her to a nearly upright position. "She wanted to be rolled down the aisle of First Presbyterian Church in a great white casket. Do you know how much those cost?"

I stared at the brown cylinder containing human remains atop the liquor cabinet. She wasn't even placed in the empty Patron bottle. "Did she like to drink?"

"Never touched the stuff."

For sure Grandma was sitting in the room somewhere with sharp knitting needles, and I should have said a prayer for her but all I could do was wonder what were my final wishes and who would carry them out? A wife? A nephew? Some nice nursing assistant doing it because I reminded her of someone she loved, or because she liked me and she'd miss me, or because I paid her?

I can see the nursing assistant in her in navy-blue scrubs under her too-thin winter jacket and tennis shoes perched at the jagged edge of the mountain, ten-thousand feet in the cold winter sky. She opens my urn/cardboard container and remembers that I had requested a song. She sings the only song she knows all the words to, the only song her mom ever listened to on the little portable record player in her bedroom. The sun is setting and the mountain glows like a pink for-tress. Her black hair blows in the wind, cheeks aflame, as she wonders simultaneously why the old people die so quickly in the winter and why her mom was so sad.

I fly into the mauve sky. The silicon chip catches the fire of the dying sun.

A crow diving through the canyon catches it in midair, carries it to her nest, tucks it between juniper twigs, feathers, and twine, and waits—waits for the day she cries, and her children see her.

UNKNOWN LEGEND

They sat at a small round table in the center of the UNM Hospital cafeteria, two cups of coffee in Styrofoam cups between them. Both were dressed in navy-blue scrubs with white name tags and the RN insignia pinned on the right side of their chests. Their conversation was barely discernible over the din of personnel and pedestrians hungry enough to wait in line for the "hot" roast-beef sandwich, salad bar, or perhaps the soup of the day—Italian Minestrone.

Dolores Slim, who was actually a little chubby, spoke in a low voice to Ruth Shorty, who was actually kind of tall. Their dark eyes sparkled under the halogen light. Wide lips, normally downturned, lifted slightly at the corners.

"When did this happen?" Ruth asked, her long fingers beginning to move as if she were a typist or a stenographer.

"Nellie told me yesterday," Dolores said. Both of her hands were wrapped around her cup, the first signs of rheumatoid arthritis apparent in her swollen knuckles.

Ruth moved her head a little closer. "Nellie's a gossip."

Dolores took a sip of coffee. "I called my brother's ex-wife in White Rock. The story was in the *Navajo Times*."

They looked around. Two white doctors in white lab coats with stethoscopes wrapped around their necks like silver snakes shuffled past in blue operating booties. They smiled at them, then returned to looking into their coffee, hearts beginning to beat a little faster.

"She was here last week," Ruth said. She carefully tore open a pack of Sweet'N Low, then a pack of Cremora. The substances sank slowly to the bottom of her cup. "She wheeled up to the nurses' station with a prescription for Demerol—for her back. She can't walk anymore."

They grinned.

Ruth took a bite of her donut. Chocolate frosting stuck to her large front tooth. Dolores said something to her in Navajo, and they both laughed. Then Ruth picked up her napkin and wiped the "shit" off her tooth.

Dolores pointed her lips to a man in line, Alfred from pharmacy. "He told me that she forged the signature on the prescription. You know her and Alfred—"

Ruth nodded, staring at her donut. "Poor thing."

The "poor thing" they spoke of was their mutual friend and clan sister, Marcella Manyhorses, who was now wanted by the federal government for robbing the Gallup National Bank. Prior to robbing the bank, Marcella had worked as an LPN with Dolores and Ruth at the Indian Hospital. She was fired, and her nursing license revoked, after stealing painkillers from the pharmacy.

"It's not her back that pains her. It's her son leaving the way he did." Marcella's son had died in a car accident on the old Highway 666 that the government renamed Highway 491, like that would somehow help. "He missed the corner on the way back from Shiprock."

"Which corner?" Dolores asked.

"You know the one."

Dolores saw it, a long black blade with a curve at the end. She nodded, took a sip of coffee, then continued. "My cousin was in the bank. She said that a white woman came in with a Colt 45 and held them up."

Ruth put her donut down.

"When the car drove off toward Window Rock, she said a blonde wig came flying out the driver's-side window. A coyote picked it up and ran off with it. The Navajo police have been tracking the coyote and the wig for two days." They giggled, then took sips of their coffee, white teeth scraping the Styrofoam. "She got away."

Ruth had seen Marcella out the second-story window of the nurses' station that day she came by the hospital. Marcella had wheeled out to her faded maroon Mercury Cougar. The sun glinted off the rickety, army-green wheelchair stamped on the back with IHS/PHS. She'd opened the trunk of the car, stood up, and tossed the chair in the back like an empty suitcase, then drove west out of the parking lot.

"She better get rid of that car."

"Even the Navajo Police could find a Mercury Cougar," Dolores said, swishing her coffee. The grounds swirled off the bottom.

"She better keep a close eye on the money," Ruth said, and she ate the last of her donut.

Dolores pulled out her compact and reapplied a bronze color to her lips. She caught an image of Marcella sitting in a booth at the Chat-N-Chew in Shiprock, her long black hair streaming over her shoulders as she read the newspaper and waited for her order of chicken-fried steak. Dolores looked at Ruth over her compact and said something in Navajo.

Ruth wiped crumbs into the palm of her hand. "I know where I'd go."

"Where?" Dolores said, snapping her compact shut.

A broad smile quickly crossed Ruth's face like a fast-moving cloud in an otherwise blue sky. "You know the place." Just below the dunes where pottery shards are covered and uncovered by the wind and time. Where once stood a tiny sandstone house carved out of the mesa. The house, they said, had been hit by a cyclone. The blocks piled up like Legos discarded by a bored child. Rattlesnakes hung from the branches of the elm tree her father had planted there nearly a hundred years ago.

Dolores nodded.

She could see her. Marcella, up on top of the red mesa, sitting on the tailgate of a brand-new Ford F-150, sipping an orange soda with a rattlesnake around her neck.

NO RAIN

It was a day like today, the color of a gray racehorse. Most everyone slept in including Mother Earth and Father Sky, and Sun had a second cup of coffee. But it was the day Caterpillar's baby was to be born. So, Mother Caterpillar had convened all of us from the four winds to witness the birth of her first child.

"How can my baby be born without the blessing of Father Sky and Father Sun?" she said, looking into the gray racehorse sky and rubbing her six front hands together. "How will she know when to come out?" she said, rubbing the temples of her green flat face as she stared at the cocoon that was as large as a grown man's finger. "And where is Bumblebee? She's supposed to bring the corn pollen."

"Have faith, Caterpillar," Hummingbird said, taking a long draught from a willow blossom.

Rattlesnake was coiled under a sunflower that stretched six feet into the sky. He stuck out his tongue, tasting the moment, and began the birth song, shaking his tail. We all looked toward the branch as the cocoon began to split.

We watched as the baby poked her fuzzy little face out of the cocoon. Her eyes looked around and she licked the air. We all gasped as she pulled her wings free from the cocoon. Wings so long we didn't see how she could have kept them contained in the tiny cocoon. Wings so black she was to be named Nightingale.

Then it began to sprinkle. Then it began to rain.

"She has blessed us all," Rattlesnake sang.

"The corn will grow ten feet tall," Caterpillar sang.

"She will make the flowers sweeter," Hummingbird sang.

Her wings came together behind her.

"She will fly to the four winds and—"

Just as she was about to take her first flight to the sun, to the moon, to Pluto—a big fat raindrop landed between her wings, gluing them together.

"It's just as I thought," Mother Caterpillar said. "Oh the bad luck."

Then we heard her coming from the South in her irregular flight pattern, bumbling along, singing a blessing song: "Oh little butterfly, I have a gift for you, from first Corn Maiden. She told me to give it to you." We could see she was carrying something as she flew through the rain that dropped around her like big wet tears, singing, "Oh little Butterfly, we have waited for you."

"Watch out," Hummingbird said and got out of Bumblebee's way.

Bumblebee flew just above the baby and opened her hands. Corn pollen landed gently on the baby's wings, drying them and turning the wings yellow. With her wings free, in a single flap she lifted off the branch into the corn-pollen butterfly sky.

Mother Caterpillar began to cry. Bumble Bee fortunately had enough corn pollen to put on her eyes to dry the tears.

Hummingbird sang, "Follow me, Yellow Butterfly. Follow me to the north. Follow me, Corn Pollen Butterfly. Follow me to the mountain. She lies sleeping, waiting for you to enter our dreams."

Our dreams—the good thoughts that are out there on the horizon, like days when the shell of this world is painted gray with swipes of white clouds that move away, repeating our stories over, and over.

We had a sweet gig for a couple months as the house band for the big casino outside Albuquerque. One evening, preshow, me and One Foot were chillin' like villains by the pool with our shades and our Jack. The sun was setting, and everything started turning pink. We'd seen it a hundred times before but . . . but maybe it was because I had on my sequined jacket a la Loretta Lynn. One Foot said it was hard to tell where I ended and where the sky began. So at the base of the Mountain That Moves, we set our drinks down and never went back for them.

—Jeannie J

Live at the House Made of Evening Light

This spring, these cicadas will offer something more, a lesson we can all use about now: how to emerge from the darkness.

—*David Rothenberg*

The music simply drifts away into the stratosphere of formal dialectic, beyond our social concerns.

—*David Hickey*

DO I EVER CROSS YOUR MIND?

What was the name of that song? It played at the edge of her mind and was a smoky tavern down on 5th Street before the crowds arrived and the sound of beer bottles landing in metal trash cans drowned out the voice and the brush of the high hat. The voice that came from some place that holds memory of all that is wonder and sadness, that sings hymns as well as old country-western tunes, a voice that slips easily from one to the other.

That song hung in the air around her and reminded her of summer evenings when she was a little girl. The dust from dirt roads has settled as the sun set behind the mesa, turning the mountain to the east pink like a giant crystal fortress at the edge of her world.

She could see a record spinning round and round on her mom and dad's Sears Hi-Fi Stereo, but the title, like so many things, had escaped her, or was leaving her in trickles like the grand river was leaving them all now. It was once wide and full, with muskrats and beavers, with toads the size of white paper plates that were eaten by bull snakes, uncoiled and stretched across the dirt road to their house.

Their house, that's where she was going, where the song was playing, where she would wander to under skies so black that the stars—well, she could almost hear them talking to one another. Sisters and brothers who had known each other for a millennium, who had fought with each other for nearly as long, who had tried to get away, only to end up every night over the desert and that old ranch-style house, laughing and sharing stories with smoke from comets rising like smoke from ashtrays.

What was the name of that song?

It smelled like alfalfa fields that had been irrigated on a summer day and the tender green plants were now exhaling brown holy water from the ditch. She took deep breaths of it as a breeze wrapped the scent of Russian Olive blossoms around her like a fine French perfume.

She was drawn by that song and laughter to the sixty-watt bulb shining like one of those stars on the back patio of their house. Moths and cicadas fluttered like drunken sailors falling on their backs, burning their wings. She would stop just outside the fence and hide behind a lonesome chamisa and watch her parents dance.

She heard the sound of worn leather boot bottoms on sand and the click of her mother's heels on the cement as she followed, two shadows, two dark flickering flames intertwined on the dance floor of the patio. Light caught their eyes as they smiled at one another and whispered.

She strained to hear what they were saying, eavesdropping, spying on them until her mom threw back her head and laughed. She wanted to join them but was afraid if they saw her their dream would tear apart, that they would remember times forgotten or that hadn't yet occurred.

Sometimes she'd curl up beside that sagebrush and sleep, waking just before dawn to find them still dancing in each other's arms. She wanted to wave good-bye and tell her parents she missed them, but she would just get up and disappear into the dawn, letting them have that time for themselves. Maybe they just needed more time for themselves.

As she walked toward the sun, the song grew fainter and fainter until it was the sound of traffic trying to get across the bridge, and then of the clock radio buzzing with the bright New Mexico sun pouring through the drapes in her own bedroom, and she woke with an old country-western tune playing in her head.

Oh, how quickly dreams fade away, like a pop song or a monsoon in the desert, and then again, how they linger like a fine layer of dust over everything.

WILL YOU STILL LOVE ME TOMORROW?

The sagebrush looks like bonsai trees, tirelessly tended to under a new moon with invisible hands that snip and look and snip and look over the course of a thousand years. I wonder, if I lie under that invisible moon for a thousand years more, could I be seen, could I be sacred fire, could I become twisted smoke and you the rain over a cracked desert floor, tips upturned like cruel lips? Could I be as patient as that cloud over there that seems to be in love with the mountain peak, so small and perfect? Every day the cloud floats toward her with strings of turquoise and shell, surrendering, then continuing on her journey, singing, "Will you still love me tomorrow?"

DIAMONDS AND RUST /
SYLVIA'S MOTHER—A MEDLEY

They met in Navajo Language 121 around 1982. Grace was studying medicine, and Sylvia was studying Grace. They were both really shy. Sylvia had been born on the reservation and Grace in Albuquerque, and they were both attending the University of New Mexico. Grace was half-Navajo and didn't know any of the language, except a few curse words and how to say, "Come and eat." Everyone else in the class, except a guy from New York, was fluent in the language, and they were there to learn how to read and write it and to meet up with other Navajos.

Sylvia noticed right away that every time Grace had to give an oral report she would break out with a new pimple, and Sylvia could understand why. Other than the deep tenderness in her voice, it was excruciating to listen to her try to speak their language. But Sylvia thought Grace was brave, brave to come into a class where she knew everyone would know more than her. (Well, *except* the guy from New York.)

So it was a relief when Grace introduced herself in Diné and Sylvia found out that they weren't clan relatives. Otherwise becoming lovers would be a double taboo. Not that it mattered. Sylvia had already fallen for Grace, who was out of bounds—a pop-up foul ball that goes up and up, and Sylvia, the catcher, would jump into the bleachers to get her. Sylvia was in love with the wandering pimple Grace tried to cover with makeup, in love with the way she pronounced dog, *łééchąą 'í*, with too much emphasis on *chąą 'í*, so that it sounded in her oral presentation like she was taking her "shit for a walk." She loved her name and the way she said it when she introduced herself, Grace wolye. Sylvia loved all of her, but it took her an entire semester before she got around to telling her. And a semester in college was like dog (or shit) years. No, they're like spaceman years, like one thousand years for every minute.

She invited Grace over to her dorm to study for the final. She listened to her entire presentation about her dog with a straight face. Even the part where Grace said, "Her shit was six years old." Then Sylvia asked her, "How do you say kiss in Navajo?"

Grace, who could be pretty serious, started looking through her notebook. She stopped when it dawned on her that she had no idea.

Sylvia, who made the best fry bread on the UNM campus, placed a big piece on top of Grace's notebook alongside a bowl of mutton stew and then showed her.

That kiss was epic—it had a long tail like a kite, or a jet stream in an otherwise empty blue sky. It was like a star that is falling, that they say is dying, but no, Sylvia said it was just starting to live.

That falling star of a kiss lasted through two more years of college. It was over more fry bread that glistened like moist lips that Grace told Sylvia she'd been accepted into med school. They both cried.

Grace said, "One day, I'll deliver our children," and Sylvia knew she could. Grace was brave like that. She would be a doctor and pull babies out headfirst, feetfirst. She'd take a knife, cut the mother open if she had to. Sylvia knew all this along with the fact that she and Grace would never have a baby. That she would soon be going back home to Keams Canyon to help her grandmother with the sheep and would never make it back.

Grace was made for this world. Her stars were made of neon, her moon a desk lamp whose soft glow Sylvia would wake to find her reading by. There was no place back on the reservation for them. Her grandmother would disown her if she found out she'd made love to a woman. She'd be cast out like dirty dishwater, and Grace would not be able to keep her big beautiful mouth shut.

And Sylvia missed home. She missed the sky that smelled like wood-smoke, and the jingle of bells on the sheep as they came back to the corral in the evening. She missed the quiet that filled her and the night sky that dripped not with neon but with stars. It was all the bravery and endurance Sylvia could muster to have stayed this long out here in the city where the only place she felt she belonged was in Grace's arms. How was it possible that the most sacred thing she ever felt was outside the Dinétah, outside the circle of their sacred mountains?

The only other time Sylvia felt she was in the right place was when they would go to the Holiday Bowl on Tuesday nights and sing karaoke. Grace would sit toward the back with a longneck beer and applaud while Sylvia sang. Some guy up front would always ask her to sing one more, and she would—Grace's favorite.

Grace always said she was born in the wrong era and her favorite song was by the great folk singer, Joan Baez, "*Diamonds and Rust.*" So she sang Grace's favorite song to her about being haunted by the memory of someone.

It was not all that surprising to Dr. Grace Forrester when she heard the name Sylvia Yazzie called over the tinny speaker at the Indian Hospital in Albuquerque. It had been fourteen years since Sylvia got on the Greyhound bus to visit her grandmother and never came back. Grace always thought she would see her again. Today was that day: "Prenatal Clinic."

Years ago, when Sylvia left and never came back, Grace drove her beat-up '71 Chevy Nova all the way to Keams Canyon to find her. She was positive something had to have happened to her, but nobody knew a "Sylvia Yazzie." Grace didn't believe them and drove all over the area until finally her radiator blew, and, just like Sylvia, she took a bus back home.

Now, all these years later, Grace looked at the name again. The name she had doodled on spiral notebooks, the name she could never forget was typed and pasted on the pale-green medical chart—Sylvia Yazzie. She picked it up, opened it. Place of residence: Keams Canyon. It was her. She could feel it. She could also feel that place near her stomach, that place that filled with heat the first time Sylvia touched her and then just burned after she'd left. On a pain scale of one to ten it wasn't even a one anymore, it was just a place that was empty, unsuccessfully filled no matter how much she worked or achieved, no matter who she tried to love or keep away. A place that was left open in her so that any old ghost could come in and wander around.

She took a deep breath. She was not that same young girl with grass stains on her jeans and long dark hair that smelled of cigarettes and wind. She was not just a girl who was left without even a good-bye. She was Dr. Forrester, a professional, and no matter that the empty place seemed to be filling with bile and she felt like throwing up the coffee she had just finished, she would handle this.

She reviewed the chart.

The patient was pregnant for the third time, having lost the two previous babies, miscarriages. Grace imagined that those were the two that were supposed to have been theirs.

The doctor in Keams Canyon had told Sylvia after her last miscarriage that she needed to see the specialist in Albuquerque. She knew the minute he told her this that it was Grace. Now Sylvia sat in the cold exam room, with the liver-colored linoleum tile, the off-white walls, the glass containers with metal lids labeled "cotton balls" and "swabs," as if you couldn't see them under the fluorescent lights, waiting for her, heart beating an irregular rhythm, which was nothing new, she'd been born that way.

When Grace was accepted into med school, Sylvia had taken the bus up Central Avenue to the uniform shop on San Mateo and purchased a stethoscope. It looked like a two-headed metallic snake and came with a black leather case that zipped. When she gave it to her, Grace placed it around her neck like a squash blossom, no turquoise, just silver.

Grace put the tips in her ears and placed the cold diaphragm that looked like a tiny drum to Sylvia's heart and listened to the beat.

"It's telling you how much I love you."

They went out to the Rhinestone. It was Cowgirl Night, and the drink special was Five Dollar Buckets of cold beer. They were cowgirls and wild Indians that night, their slick leathered boots gliding across the floor as they wove around the dance floor, two whirlwinds two-stepping and waltzing, laughing. Grace's hair, black as crows feathers, lighting on Sylvia's face as they twirled, thighs laced together dance after dance. God, she loved her, never stopped loving her. She just couldn't or wouldn't stay, but it was never a lie. She'd come back to Albuquerque one time just to find her, to see her. And she did. At the Frontier Restaurant, of course. Chance was not required when it came to finding Grace. She was in the back room, Navajo rugs hanging from the ceiling and walls, her nose in a book. Sylvia sat in the back and watched her until Grace put her books in a bag and walked out to Central Avenue and disappeared under her neon stars.

Fourteen years later she had gotten up before dawn for her appointment in Albuquerque. She prepared, changing her clothes three times as if she were going out on a Saturday-night date instead of a ten o'clock appointment at Indian Health Services. In her favorite blouse, stretched tight over her second-trimester belly, and with the top two buttons of her button-fly jeans undone, she drove the five hours to Albuquerque.

She heard the door to the room beside her open then close. A deep, tender voice asked, "How are you doing today?"

Sylvia looked in the mirror above the stainless-steel sink and saw the ghost she used to sing about so long ago.

She quickly redressed, stuffed the paper gown in the trash can, and smoothed the paper on the exam table. Before leaving out the door opposite the main hallway—where the phones rang and rang—she put her ear to the wall to hear that voice again.

"Hágoónee'," she whispered. Then she picked up the stethoscope that was on the doctor's desk. It was cold and shiny.

She put it in her purse.

I try so hard to not miss my mother. My family says I can't be calling her name, but her name is my name. I am Sylvia Rose, and my mother is Sylvia. Sylvia—it sounds like silk when you say it slow.

Because my grandmothers, aunties, and uncles don't want to call her back here to this world, they call me Rose or Junior. And I try not to think about her or to say her name. But sometimes, early in the morning when that last star that held vigil over our house winks at me, I look back, and instead of saying a prayer of gratitude for all I have, for all the beauty around me, I say out loud all the names I know for her, "Shimá, Sylvia, Naniná-bah, Mom—I miss you."

Mom, who was the best weaver in the family. She could turn the worst wool into a masterpiece. She could expertly weave a new belt between the fan for the radiator and the power steering. She could weave dough so that it was like the bread they eat in France. She could weave a story that made us laugh and cry all at once.

I know there are a thousand different ways to disappear, maybe a million, maybe as many ways as there are people on this earth. Some disappear in tiny increments, little by little. My mom was like a sand dune that was always moving, always there but always dissolving. My family said she was never the same after she returned from college, that she had left a part of herself out there on the other side of our sacred mountains. They wanted to do a ceremony for her, to make her whole again, but she refused.

The last time I saw my mom, other than in my dreams, I woke to the sound of the truck coughing and the smell of rain on the horizon. She was going to get milk and the *Navajo Times*. She was going to meet the rain.

Normally I got up early too, but for some reason that morning I didn't. I slept until the sun was just coming above the mountains. I looked out the window of our little house and saw our lopsided Ford spewing smoke from the tailpipe and greeting the low morning sky. I watched my mom go over the first hill, turn to the right, and then she was gone.

I play that morning in my mind over and over like a broken record. They say, "You're like a broken record." I say, "I'm like a sand dune, and I'm moving on. I'm going to college." Of course, my family wants me to go the other way—Phoenix or Mesa, Flag' or Tucson—but this sand dune is headed east to Albuquerque. If my mom had left a part of herself out there on the other side of Blue Bead Mountain, then I was going to go look for it.

I tell my great-grandmother when I come back, "I'll write stories for you in Diné." I tell my grandmother, "I'm going to find her."

She takes hold of my elbow and pulls me to her room. At the end of her bed is a trunk that was sealed like a tomb years ago. It's blue with faded-gold trim, numerous dents, and stickers of The Rolling Stones' iconic tongue, Jimi Hendrix, and a marijuana leaf half peeled off. My grandmother opens it. Inside the cedar-lined trunk are a pair of moccasins, some old bell-bottom jeans, a leather coat, a high school yearbook, a doctor's metal stethoscope, and a worn-out copy of a textbook, *Navajo Made Easier.*

She picks up the book and hands it to me with what look like tears in her eyes. Inside the book there are scribbles everywhere, as if my mom had spent more time doodling than studying. In the section about the proper way to introduce yourself in Diné, my mom has filled in the blanks with the appropriate clans.

At the bottom of that same page is someone else's handwriting and the question, "How do you say love in Navajo?"

Written beside that is the answer—"Grace."

PINEY WOOD HILLS

He heard the tom-tom drum just above the sound of that old hound barking on top of Cherry Mountain. He looked out from the edge of the woods and across the pasture of fescue. His face was as long and gaunt as one of granddad's old scrawny cattle headed to slaughter. The pasture wasn't much better. It was gnawed to the bone of granite beneath by the wind as it moaned across there on its way back to wherever it was it came from.

He drifted like fog down to the teepee Mama had set up next to the blacktop road. Smoke rose out of it and crossed itself with gray wisps of clouds going the other way. He realized, as he stood in front of it, that it wasn't a real teepee but made of canvas from the Vulcan Materials plant outside of town. Left over from the body bags made there and shipped out to the boys in blue.

There were two signs hanging on the side of the teepee. One read, "Closed." And the other—"Cherokee Miracle Root! Cures: High Blood, Sugar, Dropsy, Smotherin', and [a word was misspelled several times, scratched out, and replaced with] Problems of a Sexual Nature." But it was the claim after that one that made him decide he had to meet this Indian.

Mama was purifying her teepee with a Marlboro Light and thinking about packing up what was left of the root she hadn't sold that day (which was most of it) when he wandered inside. She hadn't heard the flap open and about jumped out of her buckskin dress when she turned and found him standing there, watching her. The little bells made from the lids of snuff cans that hung at the hem jingled with surprise. She threw her cigarette into the fire burning in the center of the teepee, adjusted the suede headband she wore over her long black braids, and greeted her visitor. "Oh-see-YOH."

He stood quiet as a blade of grass in a cemetery.

"That means hello in Cherokee," she said. He hadn't even bothered to take off his hat or scrape the red mud off the bottom of his boots. "I guess you didn't see the sign." Through the open flap of her teepee she could see the sky was taking on the color of an infant's cheeks flushed with fever. "We're closed for the evenin'."

"I seen a sign," he said. "Says you can bring a body back to life."

She took a deep breath and let it out real slow, showing that she was pretty tired herself and just a little put out with him. "What's gotcha down?"

"I'm dead."

He mumbled like he had a mouth full of tobacco. He'd better not spit on the floor or she would get mad. "I can appreciate that. I'm dead tired myself."

To one side of the teepee was a pine table covered with a red Mexican blanket. She picked up two black feathers and flapped them out to her sides as if she were going to fly out of there and chase the wind or go to the fish camp for supper. Smoke from a fat, laughing Buddha incense burner swirled around her like empty rain clouds.

She walked back to him and threw a piece of root in the fire. "This here," she said, holding a Ziplock baggy of a yellowish dried root out to him, "is an ancient Indian remedy. It's been passed down from generation to generation. My great-, great-, great-," she paused and counted the number of greats in her head and added one more, "great-Memaw was the world-renowned Sacajawea. My Indian name is Two Feathers That Fell from the Sky. But you can call me Two Feathers. I've been called upon to pass the ways of my people on to the white man."

She pushed the root at him. "Here you go, Mister——"

"Timothy, Timothy Roam." He didn't take the root, but he did move a little closer to her. He stood a head above her. His brown hat was stained with dark spots. Greasy black hair stuck out from under it. He filled his plaid work shirt even though his shoulders were rounded forward like he was trying to set his heart down on the ground. He had a clean shave. Either that or he wasn't old enough to grow no whiskers. His clothes were tattered, could use a wash, but he didn't smell of liquor. In fact, he had a real sweet smell about him, like Ivory soap and youth. "And I ain't dead tired, I'm just dead."

"We'll this'll take it right outta you."

"I can't sit down or lie down. All I can do is wander."

"Awful young for arthritis. I better get you the real powerful stuff."

She went back to the little pine table and put two heaping spoonfuls of yellow powder in a baggy. Over her shoulder, she said, "This'll help corns and calluses too. All you gotta do is bring it to a simmer on the stove. Drink a little for your 'somnia. Soak the rest up in a towel and put it on your feet. Those corns will drop off like June bugs in October."

He moved closer to the fire, rubbing his hands. "That's a nice fire. Bet it's warm."

Mama wasn't someone who got nervous of people real easy. Snakes—yeah! Stray dogs—maybe. People—no. She'd worked with some real roughnecks down at Parton Lumber and Spindale Mills. Met a few more while she was bartending at the Applebee's in Sparkle City. Oh sure, they wore Dockers and them funny little shoes with the fringe at the toes, but they were rednecks just the same. But now this boy here, he was making the little hairs on the back of her neck stand up and take notice.

She walked back over to where he stood in front of the fire and offered him the root, holding it up to him like she was putting a clothespin on the line. "Here you are, Mister Roam. That'll be five dollars."

He didn't say a word.

"I know that's a lot money. Especially these days, but this is a proven remedy."

He'd stopped rubbing his hands and folded them in front of him like he was about to start preaching. But he didn't say nothing, not a prayer, not a whisper.

"You want some of this or not? I'm ready to pack it up and go on home."

He looked up from the fire, and she met his eyes. They were as dark as the woods at night when only hoot owls, panthers, and those up to no good are about.

Neither one of them blinked.

"Well then—I've had all I'm gonna take of your orneriness. You can just get on out of here." She pulled back the canvas flap of the teepee and held it open for him. The fever of the sky had gotten worse. He stomped outside, turned toward the road, and yelled back, "You're a liar."

Now, she never did have enough sense to just let something go—to let it just keep on walking. "What'd you say to me?"

He walked back toward her with long strides, moving so fast it was like he had wings. "Your sign right here," he thumped it with a long index finger, "says you can bring people back to life." He thumped it again. His voice and his shoulders began to rise. "You don't know the first thing about it."

They began to circle each other, staring hard like two young ones about to commence to kicking and pulling hair. "You better take that back."

"It ain't nothin' like the preacher said it would be. There twern't no pearly gates. No bright lights. No nothin'! Except this endless wanderin'."

"Well I can fix that." She pushed him with all she had, and she had a lot. Her buckskin dress had been let out a time or two. She pushed so hard her headband flew off and she busted another seam. But sure enough he landed flat as one of her pancakes on his backside. Red dirt swirled up and matched the color of the sky. His hat took off with the wind. And when it did, she could see what looked like oil on the side of his head. She wrapped her arms around herself and held on tight.

He just stared up at the sky with those eyes that had no moon or stars in them. The only breath she heard was her own. His mouth was set in a line as straight as a razor's edge.

"Mister," she said, looking at that oil spot and bending toward him, "you got a problem." When nothing but his eyes moved, she was sure she'd broke his neck. "Are you all right?"

"I already told you, I ain't all right. And you ain't no Indian." His eyes squinted at her. "I ain't never seen no Indian with freckles."

She narrowed her eyes right back at him. "Lots of the Cherokee have freckles. And I'll tell you somethin', your problem ain't being dead, it's being stupid." She turned her broad back to him and kicked dirt like a pitcher on the mound as she started up the well-worn path, jingling with every stride, to her single wide at the top of Piney Knob. It was called Piney Knob even though there weren't any pines up there anymore, just one old hemlock that by the grace of God had survived Granddad and his clear-cutting. All the pines had been drunk up years ago.

She spoke into the wind, and the wind picked it up and took it over to him. "If you are dead, I bet it's 'cause someone kilt you!"

"Yer full of meanness. You know that?"

She stopped dead in her tracks and turned around real slow. She wasn't that surprised when he was up and walking toward her. He stopped a foot or so away. His face was as smooth as river rock, but the rest of him was as ancient as that old hemlock. The tom-tom drum began to beat.

She tried not to look at the oil spot, but she couldn't help herself. "You ain't done one ghostly thing since you arrived."

He looked up toward her trailer. "You hear that?" She couldn't. The wind blew the bells on her dress and took the story of her to the other side of the world, but she didn't know it.

"What do you hear, Timothy Roam?"

"The Cherokee. I hear 'em cryin' sometimes. The young'uns that was kilt, the women that was raped, the old ones drug naked through the snow." He covered his ears. "And the wolves and the forest that cry out for 'em to stay. But we made 'em leave. Made 'em walk. It was so cold. Their hearts broke open as wide and deep as the Carolina sky is blue. But nobody can see it."

Mama reached up and put her hand over his.

He wrapped his long fingers in hers. She touched the place where a bullet had entered an eternity ago, or was it yesterday? He can't recollect when or why he'd done it. "I wished I hadn't. But what's done, can't be undone."

The place was as hard and soft as crow feathers, and it shined as the last of the sun disappeared. She touched his smooth cheek with her other hand and rubbed it the way the wind rubs Piney Knob on a summer night when the moon's full of whatever it is that it needs to keep shining. Her heart beat to the same rhythm as the drum. It made her hand shake like she'd had too much of that remedy of hers that sparkles and winks at her from inside those bottles on the shelf above her woodstove.

She ran her fingers across his lips and then touched them with hers. In the distance the train blew its horn on its way up to Cherokee.

He whispered like a breeze that told the story of him, "You got their magic. You got their heart."

AT SEVENTEEN

I dreamed last night of Janis Ian singing in a smoky bar down by the railroad tracks where the river quietly wanders even while you sleep. The kind of place that your mama hopes you never find, especially when you should be at home with your family eating pot roast, carrots, and potatoes. I pull the collar up on the peacoat I bought at the army-surplus store. The brass buttons embossed with small anchors flash under the streetlight on the corner.

Inside, Janis Ian is on stage. She looks like a good Jewish or Lutheran housewife, or the lady at the post office, or a cashier at the Family Dollar, but she's not. And don't wake me if I'm dreaming, but she is beautiful. I nestle into a booth and order a cola fizz, because alcohol, except for large doses of tequila, makes me sleepy. I am by nature melancholy. It's a shame that such a pretty word is so undesirable, relegated to alcoholics and folk singers. It should be a tropical-fruit drink, like the ones you find at a cabana in Mexico or a smoky tavern on 1st Street in downtown Albuquerque. "Sure, I'll have one more melancholy with a twist of lime this time, please."

Then Janis asks me to come up on stage with her. My hair is long and glossy, which signals even in my REM state that this is a dream. I've worn my hair short since I was a child, except through my wild eighth-grade period when I suddenly decided to embrace being a half-breed like Cher. Oh, my bitter disappointment to find out she was Armenian and not Cherokee. Flinging my hair, I go up on stage, and Janis introduces me as her special guest, the one, the only Joan Baez, straight from a sit-in at the president's ranch in Crawford, Texas.

Janis tunes her guitar while I tell the small crowd how happy I am to be singing with Janis. We smile our thoughtful smiles at one another, Janis and I, and then we sing a "Blowin' in the Wind" / "At Seventeen" / "Diamonds and Rust" medley. The bar is as quiet as a street in the neighborhood where I grew up, where at seventeen I did nothing but

watch *Dallas* on Friday nights or hang out at the drive-in smoking pot
and getting another pimple.

But that night, tonight, I am making a difference. I can see it on the
faces of the women in the crowd, their short spiked or moussed hair
swaying to the sound of change. Their eyes fill with pride and hope, and
we shine like stars in an inky-black sky

Our fans ask, "Don't you get tired of playing other people's songs?" No. Never. We hear ourselves in the music and know it was written for us to sing. These songs are part of our story.

—*Mister*

Live at the House Made of Story

Music was my refuge. I could crawl into the space between the notes and curl my back to loneliness.

—*Maya Angelou*

I can't talk about singing. I'm inside it. How can you describe something you're inside of?

—*Janis Joplin*

GHOST IN THIS HOUSE

The awning of the ranch-style house is torn and looks like a sly grin above the brick facade. Two dogs, one a chocolate lab, the other a tall black Shepherd mix, used to run full throttle toward the gate when her daughter drove up. They guarded the home and the lone occupant as if it were a castle. A small brown patch of earth was surrounded by a sagging rectangle of split fence posts and barbwire. Their Bosque Redondo, their reservation, their home, which they'd laid claim to, not like Indians but like rugged pioneers holding against all odds.

Gravel and heat choke the weeds that have grown up in the yard and driveway. Weeds that grew like her children: one, a tumbleweed the size of a Yugo; another, mustard weed—bitter and yellow; the last a beautiful and noxious thistle. If mowed down, they joined forces with the sun and any amount of rain that came their way and returned. Roots so deep they didn't know how to die, unlike the roses under the front-bedroom window. The roses, Moondance and Belladonna Took, look as if they may not have survived their latest pruning and the long, cold winter past. They've been clinging to life for years, along with the single Winesap apple tree whose delicate blossoms had frozen so that she would not bear her small and sour fruit. The desert winds have finished herding last year's crop of tumbleweeds into the southeast corner of the yard, but there is still a hint of Russian olive tree blossoms perfuming the face of the blue sky, clear except for a scar on it's right cheek—a jet stream that trails into a future that nobody can see.

The arms of the neighbor's elm trees reach up into that sky and pray that one day they will become cottonwoods. The long black shadow of a crow still out of sight flies across the alfalfa fields, along the ditch, and like a wandering arrow sinks itself into her daughter's heart, where she stands out front at the gate looking as if she is praying, too, as the ghosts of those two dogs run past her onto the road.

BRAIN DAMAGE

My curandera told me there are people who are dead and just don't know it. Not ghosts. Ghosts are dead people who refuse to leave this world for whatever reasons. They're why some tribes burn the deceased's home with all its belongings and shoot the horse so they have something to ride away on. "What if you don't have a horse, or you've been a card-carrying member of PETA since 1983?" I had asked her. She just stared at me through a thick veil of smoke from the sage bundle that had burned in her small apartment. She made it clear that this was different.

This is someone who really doesn't know she's dead, and neither do you. You might be eating lunch with her—say, a tuna fish sandwich on Sara Lee Light White Wheat along with an iceberg salad topped with finely diced onions, chopped tomatoes drenched in ranch dressing made by "Ol' Blue Eyes" (not Frank Sinatra, but Paul Newman), and covered in Marie Callender's croutons. Or she might be sitting in her recliner that doesn't recline anymore watching *One Life to Live*, the drone of the soap opera and her oxygen condenser enough to send any soul running for the liquor cabinet, the medicine cabinet, or both. Me, I choose Puffed Cheetos. The comfort food I buy when I do her shopping every week.

I stand in her house, now, having put the groceries away. "Hi, Mom," I say.

No answer. Her eyes are closed, mouth open, wig pushed slightly back, exposing the net and wisps of brownish-gray hair. The nasal cannula that brings oxygen to her scarred lungs has slipped, and oxygen is only getting into one nostril, but the condenser wheezes and puffs just the same.

I put another Cheeto in my mouth and examine her boney hand. It's holding not only her hearing aid but also a tiny key, the kind that opens a child's diary or piggy bank.

I tap her shoulder, leaving a dusting of Cheeto on her otherwise gray Dallas Cowboys hoodie.

She opens one cataract-covered eye and raises her head like a newborn, slowly, with limited control. The other eye opens. Then they both close again when she sees that it's only me.

"Hi."

"Hello," she says. In her lap are eye drops for glaucoma. "I was just putting in my drops."

The thick yellow fluid has dried and caked on her thin eyelashes. With her eyes still closed, she holds her hand up as if she's hailing a cab, and I offer her a Cheeto like a mama bird feeding her chick a fat orange worm.

"Are you going somewhere?"

"Why do you ask?"

"You have your wig on."

My mom is always cold and the wig itches, so she usually wears a knit cap over her small brown head. A far as I know she hasn't driven since early spring when she got pneumonia. It's autumn now, and the ranch-style house is difficult to heat.

She straightens her wig and says, "Matt's coming."

Matt works for Pneumexico and delivers her oxygen. If my mom is the last person on his route, and I'm at her house, we drag the little plastic chairs to the west side, sit in the sun, and smoke a cigarette. He talks about oxygen and tanks, about capacity and weight, transport methods and regulators. I nod. There is something about him that is soothing, like oxygen itself. His passion for his job is compelling, plus I don't really want to talk about my job—waitress at an Italian restaurant—not because I'm ashamed of it, it's just that I don't have passion for lasagna *or* risotto.

He usually comes every other week, and he'd been here last week. He'd left my mom a six-pack of two-hour tanks. I ask her how she's used four. She asks me why I always have to be so suspicious. "You wanted me to walk more, remember?"

I stick another Cheeto in my mouth. "What's the key for?"

She clutches her hand. The hearing aid begins to squeal like a tiny pig headed to slaughter.

"Would you get me a cup of tea? Please."

I make her the tea she drinks year-round, Christmas Spice. I take it to her in a coffee cup that says "Ruth—The Pleasant One."

She points to the footstool. I move her crossword-puzzle dictionary—frayed and worn from years of trying to find the right words—and sit down.

"I need you to take me home."

My mom has a chronic lung disease. That's why she has to use oxygen twenty-four hours a day. Sometimes I'm sure it's affected her mind. "You are at home, Mom."

"No, *back* home. Well, to Ganado."

Ganado is where my mom went to boarding school. She's a member of the Ganado Mission Association, goes to all her reunions and keeps in touch with her few surviving classmates. The school closed many years ago, but the church remains open and is where she married my father, and the cemetery is where her parents are buried, and even though it's closed, it's where my mom wants me to place her. She's not interested in how I might manage that, or that there is the possibility that I'll have to sneak in and bury her cremated remains the way a dog buries a bone.

"Why?"

"I have to return something to someone. I've been saving it for her."

I look at her hand that is no longer clutching the key but holding on to the arm of her recliner.

She closes her eyes. "Will you take me?"

"When?"

"As soon as Matt gets here with my oxygen."

"It'll be dark before we even get there." She closes her eyes and dabs the edges with her tissue. I tell myself that if I don't take her, she'll go alone.

I wait outside for Matt while my mom gets ready. I drag the green plastic chair from the porch to the sandy west side of the house and light a cigarette, occasionally looking around the corner as if my mom could still sneak up on me.

I call Gail to tell her where I'm going. Gail is my girlfriend. Although the other night she'd introduced me as her partner for the first time. A man, who stood too close to her, assumed she meant in the food business. I call her and try and make light of my mom's plans. "You know how she is."

I'm met with silence.

"Hello," I say.

"You forgot we're invited to the pop-up restaurant in Nob Hill tonight?" Gail is a food writer, a really good one. She's frequently invited to restaurant openings and food events. Her voice softens. "Just take her keys—tell her you'll take her tomorrow—tell her you have a date. Besides, it's too late to go now."

It really is a terrible idea. Driving like a bat out of hell it'll take over three hours to get to Ganado. It'll be an additional hour if we stop to eat in Gallup at our favorite restaurant. I usually get the "Famous Biscuits and Gravy" and mom orders chicken-fried steak. "Why don't you come with us. We'll pick you up. Doesn't a Navajo Taco sound good?"

Gastro Girl, Gail's food blog, gave our favorite restaurant three and a half stars. She said the biscuit was too heavy, and the chicken-fried steak was tough. The redeeming factor to her was the added feature of shopping at the table while we ate. Sellers take turns walking around the restaurant with handcrafted items. Invariably I end up buying from a grandma just because she's cute or because the item is something I simply can't find anywhere else. Like the key holder I bought for our kitchen. It had a tiny piece of shellacked fry bread, a miniature bag of Blue Bird flour, and a little plastic sheep glued to a board with the etching, "Round, Brown, and Greasy." As I gave the artist, a young boy, ten bucks he handed me the key holder with a warning, "Don't eat the fry bread."

My stomach growls now as I look up at the mesa and blow smoke at the sun that is setting behind the Sleeping Sisters, the volcanoes on the west side of the city. Yeah, it's a bad idea.

Gail says, "I want you to come with me, like you said you would."

"She has to deliver something to a friend. It's urgent."

"Urgent? Please."

I hold back telling her I feel like fry bread or heavy biscuits. I want to watch my mom eat so much she gets full, and I don't want to go to the pop-up restaurant in Nob Hill where I don't know anyone and don't even care that I don't know anyone.

"Can either one of your cars even make it out there?"

Hers can. I think.

She waits for a response, and then right before she hangs up on me she says, "I won't expect you home."

I take off my Converse shoes and poke my toes into the sand that feels like warm flesh. I can already see the line of women and men at the pop-up restaurant waiting to take my place beside Gail. I crush out my cigarette.

I won't expect you home.

Home.

Maybe if Gail were here now, at this home, we could lie under the one functioning swamp cooler in the hallway where I read romance novels as a teenager. Maybe she could feel the part of me that got embedded in that old green carpet. Maybe she'd understand there really was a family that lived here once. It had been a home, even if it was just for a short while. And under that rattling swamp cooler I'd tell her I hadn't intended to leave a part of me, maybe the most important and best part of me, here in this dilapidated ranch house.

Or maybe if she'd just sit here in the matching blue plastic chair and watch the sun go down behind the Sleeping Sisters with her toes buried in the warm brown flesh of the yard. She, with her expert palette, could taste me on the breeze. Just like when she pops an amazing amuse-bouche in her mouth then gasps and says, "Yes, there's just a hint of Russian olive blossom and ozone." Holding tight to my hand with eyes closed, "And a note of—is it Pink Floyd? Yes," she smiles, "just above the sound of dogs barking and a mother laughing."

I think I should call her back, when magically my phone rings. I flip it open without looking. "Gail?"

"Um, no. It's Matt from Pneumexico."

"Oh, hi Matt," I say with a croaky voice.

"Sorry to call you. I tried your mom's house, but she didn't answer. I'm not going to make it this evening. There's a fire in the bosque and the bridge is closed."

"Don't worry about it. We're fine—I mean, she's fine. Tomorrow's fine."

"Okay. Tell your mom to stay inside. The air quality index is very poor."

"I will. Thanks." And I hang up. We'll have to take a different route, adding another half-hour. Yeah, it's a bad idea.

Back in the house Mom is still getting ready. Her purse and a pair of gloves are on the ottoman. Her oxygen tanks are in the corner. She has two full ones and a small one in the blue carrying bag. She might have enough oxygen to last five hours. If she doesn't breathe too much.

"Mom," I yell, knowing she can't hear me. I follow her oxygen tubing to the hall bathroom, where the door is slightly ajar.

I peek inside.

She's standing in front of the long mirror that runs the length of the double sink vanity top. She looks at her gaunt, cadaver-like reflection in the mirror. Thin wisps of gray hair drift softly over her small brown head like streaks of old snow on a sand dune. Her wig is lying on the almond-colored countertop and looks like a giant tarantula.

A place in my heart begins to hurt as I watch her struggle to hold herself upright, bracing herself with her knees against the cabinet. I watch as she picks up her partial and begins to brush it. She had always been the most beautiful woman in the room, and even now under the harsh multi-watt bathroom light, even with the lack of oxygen exchange in her lungs, I still wish I had her skin tone—a soft cinnamon-brown color.

I knock and let myself in. We used to be almost the same height. Now I tower over her. "Matt called; he can't deliver the oxygen until tomorrow."

She opens her mouth, and the partial with two large molars disappears into it. She snaps it into place with her tongue.

I turn my attention to myself. I'm not cinnamon brown, but rather a pale bisque with circles under my eyes. I pick up the spare toothbrush I leave at her house as she applies blush to her high cheekbones, then she picks up the tarantula and begins to brush it like a well-loved pet. I tell her with a mouth full of toothpaste, "Maybe we shouldn't go." She at least looks at me this time.

I spit and rinse, splash cool water on my face, and when I look up again my mom has the wig spread between her hands the way she used to do when we played "Cat's Cradle" with yarn. She pulls the thing over her soft head and wiggles it into place. I apply some of her blush and lipstick. We both straighten and take a long look at ourselves. Her wig is too big, and my cheeks are too flushed, lips too bright to be going on a road trip to the reservation with my mother. She laughs and says, "We look like Mą'ii's children."

I recall the only Indian legend she'd ever told me, about Mą'ii, the coyote. He's in the woods with his children when they come upon Deer and her fawns one night sitting by a fire. Mą'ii admires Deer's children and remarks at how beautiful their coats are in comparison to his own children, who look drab beside them. "I wish my children had spotted coats like yours." And then he has an idea. He puts his children in the fire so that the sparks will speckle their coats like Deer's children. As he stands back, like my mom and I do now, admiring them, he says, "Oh, my children, look how happy you are. You're smiling."

When my mom told me this story many years ago, she laughed and said, "You know how skeletons look, like they're smiling?"

I smile at her. The 120-watt bulbs in the fixtures above the vanity accentuate the hollows of our cheeks and the circles under our eyes. We do both look less than alive.

She applies a coat of cantaloupe lipstick. The hint of orange looks good with her wig, and I tell her so. She blots her lips and hands me the tissue.

"Mom—"

She puts her trifocals on. I want to tell her that for some reason I'm scared. But I think she already knows that. I want to tell her that she's my home and that she's still the most beautiful woman in the room, but instead I just turn off the light, and as the last of the sun eases its way in the frosted window, I think I see our eyes sparkle in the mirror's reflection. I blot my lips on the tissue and leave it behind on the counter—nearly two identical cantaloupe kisses.

"Come on, Mą'ii," I say, "it's getting late."

We drive west, up and over Nine Mile Hill and across the Rio Puerco, far past the flashing arrows of the Route 66 Casino and into an inky-black sky. We've left the moon and our good sense, if we ever had any, far behind us.

The car radio crackles, so I turn it off and listen to the sound of the road beneath us. In this old vehicle with the dry-rotted insulation around the windows it sounds like we're thousands of miles above the road, like we're astronauts, hopefully with enough oxygen to last through the night.

As we pass the Stuckey's in McCartys an hour outside of Albuquerque, the rock formations get closer to the road. This is the place that begins to echo my mother's memories. Where she begins to tell me stories: about gathering pumpkins by the full moon; about naughty children stealing candy from the missionaries; about how she fell off a racehorse once and nearly broke her neck. But tonight she's silent until we get to Grants. Off in the distance the New Mexico Women's Correctional Facility is lit up like a football stadium.

"You remember my friend Marcella Manyhorses?" she says, like she always does every time we pass Grants. Marcella is in prison for robbing a bank in Gallup. One time my mom had me drive down the state road just to sit across from the penitentiary with its high chain-link fence and shiny barbed wire.

I glance at my mom as she looks straight ahead, the glare from an oncoming semitruck reflected in her trifocals. Really all I remember of Marcella, the few times I met her at the Indian Hospital where she worked with my mom, was that she had the most beautiful black hair.

"Did you know when she was young, she won first place in barrel racing at the Navajo Nation Fair? You should have seen her on a horse."

I could only imagine what a sight she was. "What color hat did she wear?" I ask, but she can't hear me.

"Marcella took the money, fifty dollars, and bought us all sodas and so much melon and fry bread I thought we'd pop. Then there was this little old lady from Laguna who had a dead battery. Marcella made one of the boys who had been following us around all day drive us to Gallup. Marcella bought her a battery and wouldn't even take the shawl she tried to give her in return."

I nod my head and dig into the empty bag of Cheetos.

"That's the way she was." My mom looks down at her hands. "She only started taking those pills when her son died."

It wasn't along this stretch of road that he crashed, but it's where I imagine it happened—in the curve up ahead.

"He'd just gotten a job in Farmington." She always added this, like it was Marcella's son's good fortune that had killed him. "Then Marcella wrecked her car, and she started on those pills for the pain."

Mom pauses to catch her breath. This is the most she's said to me in six months. Marcella got addicted to the painkillers. When the doctor cut her off, she started stealing them from the pharmacy at the hospital. She got caught and was fired. Less than a year after that, Marcella Manyhorses walked into the Gallup National Bank wearing a blonde wig, and then she ran out with a bag of money, but not before shooting a security guard. They never found the money. They questioned everyone Marcella worked with at the hospital, including my mom. She'd told me once that she thought Alfred from Pharmacy was keeping it for her.

"Fifteen years she was in that prison," my mom says.

"Was?" I look at her too long, and the Honda drifts to the shoulder.

The rumble strips make our heads rattle, and I overcorrect, swerving into the right lane.

"Watch where you're going!"

"You told me she got life."

"She escaped."

I look in the rearview mirror. The correctional facility now looks like a constellation. My heart sinks, then plunges into my stomach as I see my mom's boney hand clutching the little key.

The reservation to me is like the dark side of the moon. For years I worried as my mom took off for "home" alone. Sometimes she would be going to meet her sisters, who, like the goddesses Spider Woman and Thought Woman, would come from two of the four corners of their world to meet at the Navajo Nation Fair.

"Where will you stay? Does anyone know you're coming? Call me when you get to Gallup," because I knew that once she got past that point there would be no reception. I'd wait for a crackling voice on her cell phone. Then I wouldn't hear from her for days.

She was free, sailing across the continental divide and down the backside of the Chuska Mountains, like we were now, going back to the place that shimmers during the day with blowing red sand and that swallows your dusty body whole at night.

We slow, and our headlights search for the turnoff into the run-down campus at Ganado. The church bell glints, and our tires crunch—not quietly enough, I think—as we drive past. The lone juniper on the hill emerges out of the dark. I drive toward it, kill the engine, and we sit on the two-track road between the groundskeeper's house and the old cemetery. The place where we've pulled up has a break in the fence with a single board at the top; the other two white-washed boards are laying on the ground. My mom has shown me this exact place several times, so that I'd remember where her parents are buried and where to place her ashes. Not that the cemetery is that large, there just aren't any tombstones.

"We're meeting her here? Jeez." It's so quiet even my whisper sounds like a shout.

My mom is looking down the hill at the old dormitories. "We lived in that dorm over there." Tonight the building, with its broken windows, is something right out of a Boris Karloff movie. It seems to be staring at us with jagged teeth. "When they turned out the lights for the night, Marcella would sneak into my bed. We'd pull the covers over our heads, and we'd dream about getting away from here."

She laughs, seeming more alive by the minute. "We were going to have handsome husbands, pretty dresses, smart children." She takes hold of my wrist. Her grip is surprisingly strong. "We were always very positive people."

I nod and adjust her nasal cannula.

She puts on her gloves and pulls her wig down over her ears like a cap. Her hearing aids, which died just this side of Window Rock, don't make a peep. She hefts the blue bag with her portable tank on to her shoulder. I turn the valve. There's no hiss of oxygen.

"It's empty."

She smiles and takes off the cannula. There are indentations on her cheeks from the tubing.

"Mom—"

She opens the car door, and all the things I'd wanted to tell her tonight become little puffs of vapor as she slides out into the cold, dark air.

Ten minutes after my mom and I bury the money in Ganado, in the place my mom said Marcella was going to pick it up, we turn right around and head home. My mom fell into what I hope is a deep sleep. I practically carry her in the house. Still in her clothes, I tuck her under the covers, secure the tube under her chin, turn on the oxygen condenser, and wait. It wheezes to life. The wig is replaced with a knit cap, and I click on her night light—a small Victorian house, the type that is supposed to be in a Christmas village. It produces a soft glow in the room cluttered with sewing she will never get to and blouses and pants that are too big for her now.

"My mother, the bank robber." I leave the room, the door slightly ajar.

It's nearly dawn, and I put on coffee. The maker spits and gurgles from the kitchen, and I collapse into the recliner. No message from Gail. Just as well. What would I tell her? "Oh—who did we meet? Um, an old friend of my mom's. She just got out of jail. Well—we didn't actually meet her—we just took the money, over ten thousand dollars that she'd stolen years before, to the arranged drop point for her. Where? The old cemetery."

She'd accuse me of lying. And she'd be wrong this time.

I get a cup of coffee and then go to the dusty bookshelf, pull out *The Secret in the Old Attic*, and retrieve the pack of cigarettes and matches I keep behind it. My cache since I was fourteen. I pick up the paper to see how far my mom had gotten on the crossword puzzle. But it isn't the *Albuquerque Journal*, it's the *Navajo Times* from September 23, ten days ago. It's open to the obituaries, and there in smudged ink, as if the paper had been read and reread a hundred times, is the name Marcela Manyhorses. According to the obituary she died on the twenty-first in Grants, New Mexico. No survivors are listed. There is no picture, but as I stare at her name, her image begins to take shape in my mind—dark eyes, white teeth, and strands of glossy-black hair that stick out from under a blonde wig.

She escaped.

I'll say.

My mom, always good at saying just enough to make me see the world a certain way. Her way. "Your father and I are drifting apart," which made their divorce sound like a cruise on calm seas. Or, "I need a little money until the end of the month," like for gas, not a house payment.

I smoke cigarettes until the sun comes up, reading the obituary over and over. Then I put it back, exactly as I'd found it.

In ten thousand years the silverfish would have eaten the money. Somehow making their way, like creatures that live forever do, into the bag with the faded gold letters, *Gallup National Bank*. Silverfish, unlike humans, don't discriminate between "ones" and "hundreds." Just like they don't discriminate between imported silk kimonos that smell of jasmine and flannel lumberjack shirts stained with sweat and tobacco.

But it hadn't been ten thousand years; it was less than two when my mother passed away in her sleep. No will, no money except mine to bury her.

The evening I take my mom home for the last time, the tires crunch on the road as I pass the church. I stop where the fence has only one rail and kill the engine.

I remember the last time I was here, that night when our breath hung in the air like questions that would never be answered. We giggled and worried, wondering if anyone could see us, if we were burying the money deep enough or too deep, and I thought, as my mom laughed and fought for her breath, that she might die right then and there, and that wouldn't be so bad because I had thought, until that night, that she was dead already.

But she wasn't. And I saw her more clearly in that dark cemetery than I ever would. She was the girl she had once been.

She spoke in Navajo, then repeated it in English. "This is the way you make kneel-down bread. I never showed you until tonight how to dig the hole. Remember, and some day you make you some bread." And she laughed.

I walk toward the old juniper that is bent even lower. Lizards scurry away, and even the crows find some other place to be as I walk up the hill. There are no headstones, only places where the ground has collapsed. I locate the large stone placed five paces west of the hole we dug that night.

The wind comes up like it always does before the sun sets. I take five long strides and kneel. The sand is warm and easily removed with the shovel. As I dig, the juniper creaks, and above that I hear a voice, speaking in a language I don't understand, soft and lilting. I look down the hill at the old dormitory. Red dust blows like smoke, and just beyond the smoke I see Mą'ii, the coyote, smiling.

I WISH IT WOULD RAIN

"What's wrong with this world is the way we think," she told her daughter. She was propped in her bed on a stack of three pillows with her Dallas Cowboys hoodie over her pink pajamas. She was feeling better today. The medicine she got at the Emergency Room the night before was working—at least for a while.

Her daughter sat on the edge of her bed and held the moment so close to her heart that even now she can see the details of her mom's expression, bright and furious.

She had fixed her mom her favorite breakfast—biscuits and gravy, with mostly gravy, white and thick. She watched as her mom mixed the two pale substances together. First cutting the biscuit into small pieces with the side of her fork, and then gently stirring the two together, methodically, the way she did everything.

Her daughter could see that now, see that her mom always had an outcome in mind, whether sewing their clothes when they were kids, making bread dough, starting an IV on a patient, or watching her children grow.

What was the outcome she had in mind that morning when she placed those words so shrewdly in her daughter's mind: "What's wrong with this world is the way we think"?

She knew that her daughter would turn them over in her mind, the same way her mom turned over the biscuits in the gravy; knew that her daughter would take these words and, like seeds, like kernels of corn, she would bury them deep in the sand, plant them and tend to them. Under the hot sun, in the days of consecutive one-hundred-degree weather, she would lean on the handle of an old wooden hoe and dream of those words, eulogize them, dance with them, and push them out into the smoke-filled sky and bring them back to her in the form of white buffalo cumulous clouds.

Did she know her daughter would stand up somewhere and say, "What's wrong with this world is the way we think"?

And if we think for just three minutes of rain clouds, just three minutes—the time of the perfect song, the time of the perfect egg, the time of the perfect story, the time of the perfect prayer—the monsoons will charge over Turtle Mountain, and rain like melting pieces of frozen tundra will drop from the sky.

Does her daughter know that she watches her now as she dances and sings and runs with the clouds that thunder over her head?

Does her daughter know that she's running with her, chasing yellow butterflies the size of pancakes made at the Frontier Restaurant, that she's dancing with rainbows and fairy tales?

With the fairy tale that we can make it rain if we think beautiful thoughts, laced with the sound of children splashing in mud puddles and the smell of wet sand and chamisa after the storm.

I hope to keep drumming until I fall over on my kit. The high hat announcing, "That's it." For me drumming is like walking, walking toward my home.

—*One Foot*

Live at the House Made of Mirage

Stories have to be told or they die, and when they die, we can't remember who we are or why we're here.

—*Sue Monk Kidd*

It takes a certain amount of courage to let the field lie fallow until you have something to say.

—*Emmy Lou Harris*

CLOSE MY EYES

It's fall now. She looks out the window of the living-room-turned-hospital-room toward the north. The window is old fashioned but sturdy, made of metal with panes that today make her think we're all living in a cage. The sun shines brightly through the window and is a lie, like a father, holy or otherwise, who says, "I'll be back soon." Like that same father who says to wait, "your reward is coming," only to find out the reward is getting out of this world, and not with your life. The sun lies like missionaries who take children away, telling the mother they're better off with someone else. And today the sky backs up these lies of the sun by allowing wind to blow the empty tire swing on the Mulberry tree, bringing its fallen leaves from the backyard to the front porch, just to recite the story of change, and that change includes death.

Her mother is sleeping, and the sound of the oxygen condenser wheezes, the automated mattress of her hospital bed inhales and exhales. She's covered in a layer of warm pink blankets topped with an Elvis Presley afghan her sister bought when she visited Graceland. Her mom's Elvis clock ticks in the background. Elvis is in his gold lamé suit, hips gyrating side to side like a metronome keeping this time for us, and at the eleven o'clock hour Elvis will serenade us with "Ain't Nothin' But a Hound Dog."

Outside the window, hummingbirds dart at the feeders on the porch, and even though it's late in the season, there are hundreds of them. Three sit on an empty branch of the corkscrew willow in the front yard and watch. They are ancestors waiting, singing arias about where they will be going with her mom.

They're the only ones she listens to now. Not the nurses or the doctors, not the wind that was an old friend but is breaking her in waves.

She believes what those birds tell her. They will care for her mother. They will show her to the place she can't follow.

They promise her that they will not leave her behind again. They will sit on that branch like tiny hooded angels even into winter if necessary, until it's time, and she believes them. She has to—has to believe that there is something far greater, even though this is all there is now, to hear her breath, to watch her wake and see that she's not alone, to see her reach her long, thin, and still beautiful arm out toward her and say, "Hey, where have you been?"

"I've been right here, Mom."

Even when I was gone, I've always been right here.

STARS

I don't want to go back. I don't want to see someone else living there, a family playing in green grass. I don't want to see the trees she planted dying, or the trees she planted surviving. No mended fences or old metal windows replaced. No shining sun on what was our .74 acres of reservation, like a trailer park this girl can't escape.

Oh, Mother, how I miss seeing your long, thin silhouette holding the screen door open as I pull into the yard through the slouching metal gate, past the one chamisa that survived bulldozing, our attempts to burn it, and you. How I miss the smell of our controlled burns, tumbleweeds aflame on late-winter days before the spring winds began to blow, cracked green garden hoses pieced together and stretched across the sand, how I miss it. We lean on the handles of rakes, cheeks red, and squint into the flames.

I didn't know it was a sacred fire.

And that the smoke can still find me now, on the other side of what is left of the river, bending over my own weeds and cracked brown clay. It drifts in, and I laugh, thinking about your tumbleweed-release program. How you would sneak to the edge of the yard at dusk holding a tumbleweed bigger than you, throw it over the fence, and watch it roll down the road. I cry remembering your dreams of the green grass that I tried to bring back, but some things just disappear, like the jet streams over my head, exclamation points as I hear you say, "I wonder where they're going." Las Vegas or Cancun, New York City or Alcatraz?

Or to that dusty place I know like the back of my hand: take a right at the C'Debca's, past the little goats and over the ditch, past the apple trees in the first curve and the old church in the second, go along the long wall of the cemetery made from lava rock and bone, and, as the road straightens out, there's an opening, a space, and your thin silhouette against an eternal sky.

Is that day glazed with the downdraft of burning Piñon?

Or will potted cana lilies be popping open bright orange?

Will that one stupid fucking swamp cooler still be clanging inside the house as we sit out on the porch, hummingbirds buzzing over our heads like flies?

Or will it be fall again, rust-colored leaves from the mulberry tree scooting across the cement driveway / basketball court like a whisper?

It was a long trip from the boarding school. He smelled of dust and horse as he stood at the entrance to their cabin. Through the open door the last shaft of daylight pointed to the rug that seemed to hang of its own volition in the corner. His wife was at the stove, her back to him. Juniper crackled, meat sizzled in the frypan, and his hunger burned the place in his stomach that ached for her, for her beauty and her sadness, all of which was in the rug. He walked toward it.

The background was light gray, the shade of the clouds before a heavy rain. The two central designs in the foreground advanced gradually from brightest white to the color of sand in the wash, to the blush of the hills, then changed abruptly from red to black. Like the sky was doing now. He saw her long fingers weaving the warp and weft as she thought of her children coming home, back over those hills outside the open door, only for night to end without them. The designs were not diamond shaped or the spinning-log motif but uniquely hers. Whirlwinds spinning in opposite directions toward the border: a sequence of black and gray zigzagged lightning. He murmured, "It's beautiful."

She came to stand beside him. Took his hat. "What does it say about me?"

He rubbed his soiled hand on his pant leg and stepped closer to the rug, looked at its detail. Gently, he felt its smooth fabric, searching for the imperfection he knew she had woven into it. It was found in the eye of the storm, a nearly imperceptible change in the color of the yarn, and slightly raised there, so that it gave the effect in sight and touch that something was holding still around the whirlwind.

"That even your imperfections are perfect."

We love to play Blue Smoke. We return and we're home. Women, who were once girls like us, bring their children to the show. The kids are embarrassed as they watch their moms dance and sing and cry. The last time we were there, the owner said that he'd found some of our things. My carillon and One Foot's wallet, Mister's leather jacket and Akeedee'naghai'igii's crossword-puzzle dictionary. Things we'd left behind over the years were returned to us.

—Jeannie J

Live at the House Made of Blue Smoke

I've tried to keep a level head. You have to be careful out in the world. It's so easy to get turned.

—*Elvis Presley*

We can't choose when to start and stop. Our stories are the tellers of us.

—*Chris Cleave*

WHEN IT DON'T COME EASY

I t was some years later when she informed me that throwing her remains over the Vegas strip was out. I was visiting her at her house, and like a raven who flies in from the great mystery, she looked at me from her periphery and said that she wanted some of her to be sprinkled or buried (I can't remember the exact words) where her parents were placed in her other favorite place, Ganado. "You'll have to sneak me in."

I assumed I'd be sneaking her in because the cemetery was so old it was full. We just laughed. I don't know what she imagined in her laughter, but I imagined Bubbles, me, and a few other people who aren't afraid of the dark or the dead. I saw us with flashlights, dressed in black, like Peter Graves on *Mission Impossible*. Cat burglars, except instead of taking, we were offering. This seemed funny, humorous at the time. Only something a Navajo like her would think up and joke about—dying, burning a body, and sneaking around with it in the dark among the dead.

But when it was that time, I was *not* going to sneak into a cemetery like a stray dog with a bone.

So I called to see if she could be placed there. My cousin said she'd find out. "She's being cremated." There was a long pause and then, "Okay, I'll find out." Adding, "You know, Navajos don't believe in cremation."

Come to find out that's why I would have to sneak her in. I still hear her laughing, one of the last little jokes between us. She could have said *something*, like, "There may be some opposition to this." Or better yet, I can almost hear her say, except she didn't, "Just don't tell anyone."

But I did, and five days later here we came, her band, her outfit of Indians—lesbians and heteros, full-bloods, half-whites, all-whites, part-Italians, part-everything-under-the-sun. In our Japanese sedans and SUVs we drove into the womb of our sacred mountains, into the Dinétah, to bury our Shima nizhoni, our beautiful mother.

The choir sang her favorite song in Diné, "How Great Thou Art." And we placed her with her parents and then had the traditional dinner. When it was nearly over it was asked that someone from the family say a few words.

The microphone squealed in the gymnasium. I looked out at her friends and our relatives and told them we brought her back here because we knew this was her favorite place of all—I know it was.

I told them that she had stayed out there for us—I know she did.

And then I repeated a story she'd told me a long time ago. I think it was really her talking, just trying to get me in trouble.

"My mom told me one time that when she was still working at the Indian Hospital in Albuquerque, Cousin Avis, who was on my Dad's side of the family, had come by work to visit her." I pointed to my dad, who'd come from Nebraska along with my aunt. Even after my parents divorced, my mom and Avis remained great friends. Avis always wore matching pantsuits. Her favorite one was purple with matching suede boots. She was short with gray hair that stuck out from under her matching purple hat. I imagine her standing at the nurse's desk at the clinic while they paged my mom.

I told the crowd, "My Cousin Avis and my mom were great friends. My mom said that when Avis left that day, one of the nurses asked her, 'Who was that?'

"My mom said, 'That's my cousin,' and she laughed. She told me, 'They probably thought, no wonder her husband left her.'"

The gymnasium was silent.

Now what kind of story was that for me to tell right then?

But then I laughed. The whole crowd laughed. Dad laughed. And I know before she walked off, disappearing into the Place That Shimmers, laughing, shaking her head and smiling, she said, "That crazy girl."

STAIRWAY TO HEAVEN

They said you were born on the day the president was shot, but I'm here to set the record straight—Eerbie Shorty was born in the summer when the sunflowers were twelve-feet tall and the blooms as big around as dinner plates used by Queen Elizabeth. Eerbie Shorty was supposed to be the next great leader of our band of the Diné, who had moved to the east side of Blue Bead Mountain, who had dared to cross the great river and lay claim to land just this side of the Camino Real and that side of the Santa Fe Railroad. The trains still hum tunes about him as they wander back and forth across the Dinétah.

Eerbie Shorty, who defied his own name and grew to be six foot two, died of AIDS in 1983 at BCMC hospital. He died without anyone but me and the male nursing student who'd fallen in love with him knowing that he was our leader. But we did record some of his visions.

The last one he told us as he lay with tubes coming out of his lungs and arms, his skin a pile of bruises, his eyes little pinpricks of light in the gray room. I rubbed the top of his head and felt the indentation there. He said that was where he had been hit over the head with a beer bottle in 1978, a Budweiser long neck, but I knew it was the hole the Ancient Ones have, the ones that can still talk without speaking, the ones that can fly.

"You know, little Cuz," he said, struggling to keep his eyes open, "I can see faces in the stars now." He stared up into the squares of the asbestos-tile ceiling. "I think I see Uncle Edward. You don't know him, but he's always full of jokes. Oh Jeez, there's your parents dancing—don't they ever get sick of that song? Oh, oh, there's my favorite auntie, she's making fry bread. Can you smell it? And I think someone told me that up beyond Jupiter, that's where our grandparents live now. They have a huge hogan and about five thousand children. Yeah, there's our grandmother, she's riding a white horse. Damn, she looks good. There's Shicheii, he has a new Ford truck he's learning how to drive."

Eerbie turned away from the asbestos tile stars and looked at me. "Guess where I'm going to live, little Cuz."

The nurse closed his eyes and my tears dropped onto the white sheet as I said, "Behind Uranus."

"Look for me there."

And we did, the male nursing student and I, every Tuesday night at the university observatory. We'd ask the assistant to point us in the direction of Uranus and then giggle softly.

But we aren't Ancient Ones. We can't see faces in the night sky.

I can't find the huge hogan behind Jupiter with five thousand and one children.

But as we walked back to the car and the wind swirled, we were like stray dogs who live in back alleys, our ears perked up, and we know you saw us as we drove away with "Stairway to Heaven" playing on the one good speaker of my Ford Falcon.

YOU'LL THINK OF ME

My mom carefully unwrapped and placed two dinner plates on the green tarp we'd laid out on the dusty fairgrounds turned flea market. She had gotten them by saving S&H green stamps for the first five years of her marriage. Now that she was in the third year of her divorce they were for sale. The box we brought them in had "$10.00" written on an upturned flap that blew in the late-morning breeze.

My mom and I were selling things. We felt like real old-timey Indians sitting on the back of her Ford, sipping soda and coffee and trading our things for money. There were among other things: my hand-sewn confirmation dress, a really awful green, not like the new leaves on a geranium but more like those same leaves in need of water; a lopsided table lamp; shoes that looked like our feet were still in them; and our dinnerware, originally a setting for a family of five, but now only four and mismatched, all except the teacups. That's because they were like the paper towels that hung by the sink and were only for show.

Although it was not real china and they were not delicate, I thought they were exotic. The pattern was a cobalt-blue tranquil scene of a river, its two sides traversed by a wooden bridge with a willow hanging over the gently flowing water. I imagined just beyond the blue border of the plate there were lovers carving their initials with sharp steak knives into a tree.

As my mom and I sipped our drinks, beginning to get sunburned, a small woman holding the hand of a little boy stopped at our space and picked through the clothes, finding none that were her size or style and none for the little boy. Then she saw the plates in the cardboard box. My heart sank a little as she let go of the boy's hand and kneeled down to take a closer look. My mom slid off the trunk of the car and went over to tell her that there was one bowl and a saucer missing. She picked up a plate and pointed out a chip, then knelt across from her, unwrapped the teacup, and handed it to the woman in the long skirt and flat shoes.

Then she handed her a saucer. The woman asked my mom something in Spanish, which we don't speak. My mom just unwrapped another cup and tried to demonstrate that there was no saucer by placing it on her long brown hand. The woman said something else, and my mom said they were good plates.

The little boy was running in the aisle between spaces with a toy on the end of a stick like a kite. The woman spoke to him, and he came and walked around our stuff as my mom and the woman, who was probably twenty years younger, knelt with the teacups.

When I think back now on our dishes, I don't see our family around a dinner table. I see my mom smiling at the little boy and two women kneeling on the ground like relatives. They could have been making tortillas or kneel-down bread. They could have been sitting in a park on a sunny day on a green lawn, watching their children play.

My mom ran her finger around the blue border of the saucer and said, "There's a chip."

I was hoping the woman would think the dishes were too old fashioned, but she made an offer of four dollars, and I countered with eight with some finality, even though they weren't my plates, not my green stamps meticulously saved and taken in little books to a store in exchange for something beautiful to set on a table for a family.

My mother nodded at her, and together they rewrapped the newspaper around the dishes, black ink staining their fingers.

CHANGE

Some families are like grand oaks that grow steadfast in the same place, generation after generation. Others are like weeds, tumbling and crashing into each other, disintegrating then rising again the following summer without any nurturing and just a whisper of a prayer. Some families are like roses grown in the desert, requiring laughter to make them real.

When I was a kid my bedroom window faced east, the sun illuminating the small room I shared with my older sister. The drapes, special ordered from JCPenny, glowed like an orange soda, like contentment.

But contentment, akin to peace, is fragile, much like the desert floor that can become a torrent of water during monsoon season. Lightning and ozone all that's left behind of what had been planted. When disaster strikes and wipes out your fields, your home, where do you find the strength to plant again? Who do you speak to, the sun or the moon?

I got the answer as I was sitting on the edge of the hot walkway in front of our house in my cheap drugstore sunglasses staring at the sun, daring her to blind me. A gust of wind blew sand in my face and then whispered in my ear, "Don't let it die."

I looked around. On the porch in black containers were two rose bushes my mom had bought weeks, maybe months ago. Occasionally I would give them water and return to sitting on the edge of the walkway, my toes curled up in the dead grass. I thought of the old tiller my dad had left behind, then eyed the spot where we had thought of planting them beneath my bedroom window—now a patch of hardened soil since the rain gutters had fallen off the house.

I got up and dragged the tiller from the garage and down the cement walk. We sounded like a metal demon, a storm on the mesa. Mom came to the front door.

"It's time," I said. "We've got to plant those rose bushes—they're gonna die."

She studied the old Sears tiller. Rusted, naturally decayed, cocked to one side, it looked dangerous and harmless at the same time.

She came outside, taking hold of one handle while I took the other, and we completed our procession to the small patch below the window. I checked it for gas then pulled the drawstring over and over. Sun watched us from a distance as we took turns trying to start it until our skinny arms burned and we gasped for air.

Wind came up, blew sand in our eyes, and yelled, "Open the choke."

Mom flipped the switch, I pulled the string, and the old tiller sputtered to life.

We looked at each other. "Flaps up," I said, and I pushed the throttle all the way down. The tiller lurched forward, dragging us behind it. It was like a wild mustang glad to be out of the corral, knocking us off the handles and bucking from hard-packed ground to house, kicking up dust and tearing the stucco off the wall.

Choking on exhaust, I got a hold of the handles and yelled over the noise, "Disengage the engine!"

I looked at her, my copilot, doubled over with laughter. "Mom, flaps down!"

She reached the lever. The tiller sputtered, shook one last time, coughed, and died. I pulled my sunglasses off. Rings of dirt surrounded my eyes, which only made mom laugh harder. I stared at the holes in the side of the house, horrified at the damage we had caused. If Dad were here, he'd kill us.

But he wasn't here.

Then something akin to sadness rose up in me and erupted painfully into laughter.

My mom looked at me and without a word went back to the garage, got the shovel, and began digging. Sun pulled a cloud over her face as we dug two holes, wide enough and deep enough for our rose bushes. We poured water in the holes and watched it seep slowly into the soil. It was a grand burial, the smell of moist soil rising like smoke, as we patted the ground.

For years we had so many roses that at times the branches sagged with the weight of their grace.

And still, after all these years, on some hot summer days when the wind begins to blow, I wonder what it's saying. Maybe nothing. Maybe it's just blowing a memory back to me, a memory of me and my mom standing in the desert, laughing like two black crows. Laughing just to laugh, again.

After all those years of touring and standing in the background or next to the speakers, Akeedee'naghai'igii went deaf. She kept playing though, feeling her way through the songs like always. Keeping us in time. Finally one morning we got a call that her hearing aids were ready for pickup. We drove to the audiology clinic in our new Transit-250 that purred like a kitten. We waited outside in the parking lot. When Akeedee'naghai'igii walked out, she smiled and said,

"I can hear again."

—*Mister*

Live at the House Made of Dawn

Memory is the way we keep telling ourselves our stories—and telling other people a somewhat different version of our stories.

—*Alice Munro*

DUST IN THE WIND

Out on the horizon there is a place where the warp of red sandstone meets the weft of blue sky. Strands of asphalt are woven with threads of dirt road. Long brown fingers wipe a child's greasy smile with a white paper napkin and then place that smile in the rug she is weaving, along with the sound of a barking dog, thunder, and the soft whisper of rain on the sand dunes.

On days when my memory and my good thoughts are like dust that flew away, I go outside and listen to the wind. She carries our stories back to me across wide waters and sand dunes in the form of small white clouds that race toward me and burst through the wooden screen door like a child chasing her dog. In the waves of wind that bend the huge elm trees around my home, I hear my cousins laughing. In the center of those clouds is rain and the sound of our mothers gossiping with one another again. I smell wet dirt and sagebrush.

I look down and see that I've tracked mud onto the rug. My footprint is the place I call home. The place where we are woven is no longer the mistake but the place in the rug that makes it perfect.

WILD HORSES

My mom told me a story once about a pretty dress she made in home economics. We sat together on the couch we'd picked out years ago at American Furniture. The couch was the color of our desert sky as it moves off the mountain and into the forever. We fell together in the middle and touched shoulders. She was warm and small and smelled like Caress soap. She looked at the TV and her friends of many years from *One Life to Live*. But her brown eyes told me that she was far from this room, the cataracts momentarily eclipsed by stars as she opened one of those doors from the past that she had nailed shut. And even though her long brown hand rested on her thin leg, she pulled me like a kite, by strings attached to my heart, through that door, and I saw where she was born.

If I close my eyes, I can hear her voice so soft and distant that it sounds like some old song on a long-forgotten AM radio station. And although our oral history is a little fuzzy around the edges, I see her clearly, walking toward me, silhouetted against a landscape of blowing red dirt, rock, and bone. As she comes closer, I see the dress. It is off-white with delicate blue flowers—like asters or poppies, like the color of her wedding china, like the blue that wraps itself around the edges of rain clouds. It's fitted around her short waist, less so over her hips.

Skinny brown legs stick out, and there's a scab on her right knee. The traditional necklace of turquoise and silver is replaced with a sheer pink scarf worn around her neck and tied fancifully at the side. Her straight brown hair has been cut, curled, and sprayed. All signs of her bloodline are coiffed away. She smiles into my imaginary camera and has been captured on the back of my mind like an Indigenous Jackie O.

Her scarf blows in the wind. Elm trees line the wash to the west of the mission boarding school, "Home of the Panthers," the Presbyterians, and her. Her books are held to her flat chest, and she hums a tune she heard on the radio in the basement while she helped with the laundry. I follow her as she leaves the faint scent of dust and soap behind like the tracks of beetles in the sand. Her back is straight as she walks through the campus alone. Skipping, nearly dancing along the sidewalk. The merciless blue sky, the color of a robin's egg fallen from its nest, surrounds her and, through the wind, begs her forgiveness. At the edge of the horizon that is so vast sometimes even the black birds are frightened to fly toward it, smoke rises and signals for her to come home.

As we sat together on that couch, her hands folded and unfolded like a prayer being interrupted over and over. She did this my whole life, gripped and ungripped, steering wheels of our Ford LTD, her Pontiac Le Baron and Honda CRV. Her fingers moved while she watched TV or talked on the phone as if she were knitting an imaginary blanket. One with a pattern that would someday make sense.

And then her hands stopped as she told me, "There were these boys who were always teasing me. You know how boys are? They came up from behind."

No, I want to say.

No, I want to yell, don't take this from her.

"They put a bag over my head and dragged me to the wash and pushed in. My dress was ruined. I never wore it again."

She never wore it again. It's still hanging in some musty old closet with the door slightly ajar. I know, because we dared to go back, even though she'd told me not to. "Walk through and don't look back," she said so many times when the decisions were hard.

Now I have a life filled with doors. Blue doors faded from facing the sun day after day. Squeaky doors that tell people you're trying to disappear. Wooden doors that are hand carved but missing the key. Metal doors that are supposed to keep us safe. And a sliding-glass door that sticks with sand in the tray, so I stand on this side of it and look out onto what used to be a lawn with a swing set and think of you, Mom, and the door you are now.

Sometimes in my dreams—or at least I say "it was a dream"—I see the last door you walked through and didn't come back. It's so cliché and clearly unimaginative—a sheer cloth covers the opening, and it flaps in a wind that I can't feel and is illuminated by a light that is not a sixty-watt bulb, or halogen, or a one-eyed Ford. And when I dare to get close enough to the opening, I see that the cloth has delicate blue flowers. Are they asters? Are they poppies? I don't know. But it reminds me of a bedsheet that hung on the line a thousand years ago that smelled like a day that has no memory. And hanging behind it is that dress—dry and clean.

The dress you were to wear as you crossed from being an Indian into becoming white. You wear now.

Your hair is long and straight like your back, this world no longer compressing you. And in the distance, against a sky that is the same color as those little flowers, is high corn growing and smoke coming for you. Always coming for you from a little stone house at the base of the red mesas. I hear you whistle for your favorite horse as you kick off those useless shoes that hurt your feet and ride away toward the edge of this world—toward home. Your skinny brown legs clutch the horse's fat belly. Your head's bent forward into the wind, the pink scarf curling and uncurling like a snake behind you. Until it flies off, far away, a twirling ribbon of hope.

It is finished in beauty.

—*Cynthia J. Sylvester*

All the stories collected here were written by the author. The inspiration for these works is my family and my community; it is music and the elaborate healing ceremonies of the Diné—ceremonies comprised of thousands of songs and poems and stories and artwork; ceremonies that bring a family and community together for healing.

Some stories in this collection were previously published, and I am grateful to the following publications for their support:

> *ABQ in Print*: "Sympathy for the Devil" and "Unknown Legend"
> *Apricots and Tortillas: An Anthology about Growing Up in Albuquerque in the Postwar Years*: "Change" (published as "Two Crows Laughing") and "Flying High Again" (published as "Legend of the High Noon Moon")
> *As Us*: "Stairway to Heaven" and "Diamonds and Rust / Sylvia's Mother—A Medley"
> *bosque (the magazine)*: "Piney Wood Hills" (published as "We Wander"), "Wild Horses," and "Into the Mystic"
> *Conclave—A Journal of Character*: "The Last One"
> *DimeStories*: "Hotel California"
> *Leon Literary Review*: "Help Me Make It through the Night" (published as "Dark Cloud Is at the Door") and "(Sittin' On) the Dock of the Bay" (published as "The Mountains I Become")
> *Lunch Ticket*: "Do You Wanna Dance?"

"Where Eagles Fly" is adapted from the Tlingit song written by Among-the-Brant. Among-the-Brant's poem "Carrying My Mind Around" was published in *The Sky Clears: Poetry of the American Indians* by A. Grove Day.

Thank you to the University of New Mexico Press and the Lynn and Lynda Miller Southwest Fiction Series.

With a heart full of gratitude, I acknowledge and thank the writers that sat with me through the years in cafés and classrooms, homes and offices, the backroom of a service station in the Northeast Heights, and a few bars. Where we all worked on our craft together. I so appreciate the mentors who helped me examine and reexamine these stories and poems, who encouraged me to "write it in blood." Lisa Lenard-Cook, Betsy James, Lynn Miller, Joy Harjo, Summer Wood, and Hilda Raz. Thank you to the New Moon Poets who saw this manuscript at the Taos Writers Conference way back when. Thanks to my writing buddies, Lynda Miller, Lynn Miller, Ellen Barber, Harriet Lindenberg, and Tanya Brown. To the *Plume* network, *DimeStories*, and my dear friend Jenifer Simpson. To my Wallie critique group. Special thanks to Kristin McGuire and Tina Carlson for the eyes, heart, and talent you brought to this book. To Tony Plebani and Pax Garcia for helping to find the structure for this book by performing *Stories That Rock* with me. To my best friend, my wife, my love, Kim. Thank you for your unending support and for never allowing me to stop believing in me. And to the ancestors who whispered to me in the wind.

Thank you all!